FiREWaLLERS

Simon Packham was born in Brighton. During his time as an actor he was a blind fiddler on HMS Bounty, a murderous vicar, a dodgy witness on *The Bill* and a variety of servants including Omar Sharif's personal footman and a coffin carrier for Dame Judi Dench.

He now writes fiction and lives in West Sussex with his wife, two children, a cat called Pax, and a number of hamsters.

comin 2 gt u was his first novel for children, and received great praise for its thrilling narrative, and exploration of cyber-bullying.

The Bex Factor hilariously questioned our fame-obsessed society's love of reality TV.

Selective mutism and stand-up comedy disguised a poignant tale of friendship and grief in *Silenced*.

Firewallers is Simon's fourth book for Piccadilly Press.

Find out more at www.simonpackham.com and read an interview on www.piccadillypress.co.uk

FiREWaLLERS

SIMON PACKHAM

PICCADILLY PRESS

For Ruth and Melissa

First published in Great Britain in 2013
by Piccadilly Press Ltd,
A Templar/Bonnier publishing company
Deepdene Lodge, Deepdene Avenue, Dorking, Surrey, RH5 4AT
www.piccadillypress.co.uk

A catalogue record for this book is available
from the British Library

ISBN: 978 1 84812 307 6 (paperback)
ISBN: 978 1 84812 308 3 (ebook)

1 3 5 7 9 10 8 6 4 2

Pr[......]in the UK by [......]4YY

Part One

Whenever I think about it – and I've kind of been training myself not to – the first thing that pops into my head is the swoosh and swirl of the sea; like some gigantic cappuccino maker, it was the soundtrack to everything.

If that didn't drive you mental, the salty air, which would have defeated even the latest anti-frizz serums (if commercial beauty products hadn't been strictly forbidden, that is), made for a never-ending cycle of bad hair days.

And then, of course, there were the Firewallers.

Work Experience

But I suppose I should begin with work experience. And guess what? It sucked. There's probably more than one person at St Thomas's Community College who'd tell you it was all my own fault. As a certain Mr Colin Catchpole BA so humorously remarked, 'There's Greenwich Mean Time and then there's Jess Hudson Time'. Maybe I *did* leave it to the last minute. Maybe the kids you'll see opening their record GCSE results in the *County Times* next year had fixed their dream placements at the vets/law courts/mortuaries/software development companies (delete as necessary) months ago. But it still wasn't fair that I'd spent four whole days getting up at stupid o'clock and squeezing myself into a carriage full of sweaty commuters while Dad made feverish love to his latest laptop in the seat opposite, just because the only place that would take me at such short notice was his dumb bank.

Anyway, it was my last day, and I was congratulating myself on making it through until lunchtime without dropping dead of boredom when . . .

Oh wait, did I tell you how hideous I looked? Mum said there was nothing 'suitable' in my wardrobe, so she dragged me round town on Sunday afternoon, refusing to top up my phone until I'd agreed to a grey pencil skirt, black court shoes that turned walking into a mystic art and a disgustingly white bra, which according to her was 'bog standard issue' with the straitjacket blouse. And then Dad had the cheek to tell me to 'go easy on the make-up'. If I hadn't insisted on taking my *Where's Wally?* sports bag, I would have blended into the background just like him.

Dad doesn't do surprises, but he was about to break the habit of a lifetime. He doesn't do lunchbreaks either, but he always let me wolf down my Starbucks panini in his little glass office on the third floor. And even though he didn't say much – just muttered occasionally as he pummelled his keyboard – it was nice to spend a bit of time with him for a change.

I'm still not sure what he did exactly; on the door it said *David Hudson, Senior Analyst.* All I knew was that he was in the middle of some deal or other – and that judging by the enormous black suitcases under his eyes, it wasn't going particularly well.

That's why I decided to give him a laugh, bursting into his office without knocking and waving an imaginary gun. 'OK freeze! Just hand over the money and nobody gets hurt.'

It was a stupid joke. Apart from the rubbish American

accent, it wasn't the sort of bank you robbed anyway. According to most people, it was the sort of bank that robbed *you*.

Dad certainly wasn't laughing. And why was he fiddling around under his desk anyway? All I could hear was a dull thud and that swear word he only used when he thought I wasn't listening. (Like I didn't hear it every seventh second at St Thomas's.)

'What's up?' I said, quickly concealing my two-fingered revolver in a fist. 'What are you doing?'

'I could ask you the same question,' said the curly-haired guy in the Arctic Monkeys T-shirt who popped up from behind Dad's desk, rubbing the top of his head. 'Who are you anyway?'

I remembered just in time that I was undercover. Incredible as it sounds, there were actually people who would have walked over broken glass to do work experience at Dad's bank. That's why only Brian Simkins, my mentor for the week, knew who I was, in case it looked like favouritism.

'I'm Jess,' I said, suddenly clocking that underneath the geek chic exterior he was really quite cute. 'Who are you?'

'Steve . . . Steve Cook,' he said, slipping a screwdriver into his plastic toolbox. 'IT support, not that it's any of your business.'

The first flirtable bloke of the week and he had to go all defensive on me. 'Yeah, sorry about that,' I said, doing that thing Ella taught me where you suck in your cheeks to make dimples. 'I'm on work experience. Someone told me to wait here for Mr Hudson. Do you know when he'll be back?'

'Soon,' said Steve, checking his watch and heading for the

door like he couldn't wait to get shot of me.

'Great band,' I said.

'What? Oh . . . yeah,' said Steve, realising I was checking out his T-shirt. 'Seen them live three times.'

'Nice one.'

He could have done with a decent moisturiser. The ghost of a smile flickered across his dry, chapped lips. 'Anyway, I'm finished here. Just a bit of routine maintenance. I'll leave you to it.'

'Nice meeting you, Steve. Pity it's my last . . .'

I watched him hurry towards the open lift and throw himself through the doors like Indiana Jones. I wasn't that hideous, was I? Why did any half-decent bloke find conversation so challenging, when the ones you couldn't care less about wanted to talk your face off?

And then my phone went *again*.

Maybe Dad was texting to tell me where he'd got to – except of course he barely knew how. Who was I kidding anyway? Dan Lulham had been pinging non-stop texts at me me for the last three days. And they all said pretty much the same thing.

luv u baby. pleez!!! take me bk
soree I hurt u. pleez cum bk
u and me were gr8 together
what can I do 2 gt u bak?

Yeah, I know. How did I ever get involved with somebody who still used text speak in a non-ironic way?

OK, brief update, so listen carefully. Daniel Bergkamp Lulham: spotty chin, crap taste in music. Good kisser, great hair. The love of my lunchtime. We got together at Ella's party and almost made it to our six-week anniversary. If you're ever unlucky enough to meet the little maggot, do yourself a favour and tell him to get stuffed.

They say that truth is the first casualty of war. It was certainly the first casualty of the war graves trip. Long story short: whatever he was doing to Natalie Corcoran in the mock-up of the trenches, it was *not* demonstrating First World War resuscitation techniques. Now Natalie had dumped him too. And surprise, surprise, he wanted me back.

The dumb thing is, I was half thinking about it. You know what it's like, a two-timing rat in the hand is worth half-a-dozen Prince Charmings in the head – especially with the summer holidays looming. And I was just about to text back when —

'Sorry! Sorry, Jess. You haven't been waiting long, I hope.'

'Dad, are you OK? You look . . .'

He looked terrible. Red-faced and shimmering with sweat, he took a quick swig from his bottle of Evian and homed in on the computer. 'I'm fine,' he said, tapping in his password.

'What have you been doing anyway? You never said you were going out.'

'Oh, you know,' he said, relaxing visibly when he heard the Windows theme tune. 'Just . . . stuff.'

It was the same answer I came out with whenever he asked me what I'd been up to at school. Dad was so preoccupied with work that I knew for a fact he'd hardly left his office all week. 'Yes, but where were you? I've been here for hours.'

You see the thing about my dad is that – unlike Dan Lulham – he finds it almost impossible to tell lies. He stopped typing, barely able to look at me through sad, droopy eyes that were in urgent need of a revitalising roll-on. 'We weren't going to say anything – not yet. And if you don't mind, I'd prefer it if you kept it to yourself for now. You see, the thing is Jess . . .' He drummed out the rhythm of galloping horses on his glass desktop. 'The thing is . . . there's something I need to tell you.'

I was already wishing I hadn't asked. 'It's OK, Dad. I know you're busy with that Russian thing. Why don't you tell me tonight, yeah?'

'No, no, it's all right. You'll probably find out soon enough anyway.'

What happened later was absolutely horrible. So I think it's kind of interesting that the thing that still gets to me, the thing that still jolts me back to consciousness in the middle of the night, is when I remember what Dad said next.

Things Can
Only Get Better

'I expect you've noticed that your mother and I have been having . . . problems.'

'No,' I said, conveniently ignoring the Sunday afternoon silences, the Saturday night bickering and Mum's mantra about Dad never having time for anything 'except bloody work'.

'It's probably *mostly* my fault,' said Dad. 'This job doesn't get any easier you know.' He stole a glance at his computer screen. 'That's why Margaret thought we should see someone.'

The only time he called Mum Margaret was when she offered advice on his driving technique.

'You don't mean a solicitor, do you, Dad? I mean, you're not getting . . . ?'

'No . . . No, no, no. I mean . . . *no*. We've been seeing a marriage counsellor, that's all.'

There were plenty of two-bedroom kids at St Thomas's. I just didn't fancy becoming one. I couldn't see any advantages in bed and breakfast at your dad's place every other weekend; although according to Ella it was why she was allowed so many parties.

'I've been shooting off to East Croydon every Friday,' said Dad. 'Well, you know what the trains are like; getting there and back in an hour forty is a tall ask.'

'Why can't you just talk to each other? You don't need a stupid counsellor.'

Dad smiled. 'That's what I thought at first. But Tricia's actually very . . . insightful. She's helped us identify some of our most destructive patterns.'

Dad laughed like a drain at those telly programmes where a few questions from a 'trained therapist' about the victim's childhood were enough to cure any freaky eater/chronic hoarder/habitual gambler/selective mute (delete as necessary). It didn't sound right when he went all holistic on me.

'Dad, *please*.'

'Don't cry, Jessica. We'll sort things out, I promise.' He lowered his voice, almost seeming to check the filing cabinets for hidden microphones. 'Look, I'm sure I don't have to tell you this, but it wouldn't be too great for me if what I've just told you came out here. The partners aren't exactly sympathetic about anything that might interfere with work.'

'I don't care about that. All I want is for you and Mum to —' And I would have carried on sobbing if two sharp knocks hadn't announced the arrival of the most tedious man on the planet.

Dad looked relieved to see his trusty assistant. 'Ah, here's

Brian. I'm sure he's got something interesting planned for this afternoon, Jess.'

'Yes indeed,' said the man sprouting copious clumps of hair from every possible part of his body except his head. 'I thought I'd try and make a better job of explaining mergers and acquisitions while we bind those new pitch books.'

I offered up a silent yay.

'Did you get those figures for me, Brian?' said Dad.

Brian nodded and handed him a sheath of documents.

'And?' said Dad.

'Looks like you might be on to something.'

'I'd better get down to it, then,' said Dad wearily. 'I'll see you in reception at seven, Jess.' He leaned towards me across his paper-strewn desk. 'And please don't worry about . . . you know. Things can only get better, I promise.'

And the sad thing is, I think he actually believed it.

I was too upset about Mum and Dad to do anything but shove another page in the photocopier and put on my listening face.

'You see a derivative is basically a contract with certain conditions attached. Now you can either use them as a way of . . .'

Brian Simkins could have won Olympic gold for boring, but we did have one thing in common: we both thought the world of my dad. Brian owed him big time. He'd been off last year with 'stress' and Dad had persuaded human resources to create a special job for him.

'I'm afraid we'll have to come back to this later, Jessica,' he said, piling up a mountain of a freshly bound pitch books and balancing them under his chin. 'Your father wants me at the meeting for moral support. He's really going the extra mile on this Russian deal. The clients don't like it of course. And I don't suppose the partners are that thrilled either. It's actually very brave of him. The whole thing could all blow up in his face.'

Brian must have interpreted my miserable expression as a look of disappointment.

'Don't worry, we can still go over derivatives again. In the meantime, I've arranged for you to spend an hour or so with one of our IT chaps. Perhaps if you're lucky, young Steven will show you how the firewall works.'

I wasn't that bothered about the firewall, but I couldn't help wondering if young Steven was the same guy who'd been so desperate to get away from me in Dad's office. Surely an hour in my company would show him the error of his ways. Shallow as it sounds (and I've been called worse things, believe me) my state of mind was already improving.

Maybe Dad was right. Maybe things could only get better.

DJs and Canapés

There were few signs of life in the pokey office on the lower ground floor – just a deserted workstation, a dead can of Coke beside a half-eaten cheeseburger and a noticeboard bulging with health and safety procedures and assorted photographs of a woman with a fake tan and a smile to match.

Brian checked his watch for the forty-fifth time and made annoying clicking noises with his tongue. 'I know it's probably against every child protection initiative in the book, but I really should get to that meeting, Jessica. Your father could do with some support up there. Would you mind waiting on your own until young Steven arrives?'

I tried not to sound too delighted. 'Yeah, no worries. I'll be fine.'

'I'll see you in an hour or so,' said Brian. 'Maybe later I could talk you through how a hedge fund works.'

You've probably realised that I'm not one of those burst-a-blood-vessel sports nuts who stampede across the school field trying to thwack the hell out a hard white ball with a long stick. I prefer my sporting challenges a touch more sophisticated. Ask Ella about that spitting game we invented in Year Nine. So, after I'd finished snooping round his office doing my Sherlock act (he was clearly a one-legged man with a passion for tropical fish, a mild nut allergy and a sister in Skegness), I came up with a brand new sport of my own.

Kicking off my court shoes, I picked up the deceased Coke can and dragged a black swivel chair to the far end of the office. Sometimes the simplest ideas are the best. I sat in the chair with my legs scrunched up, pushing hard against the wall to propel myself backwards at death-defying speeds. The aim of the game was to chuck the Coke can in the wastepaper basket before you got to the other side of the room. And because I'm a lot better at colour coordination than the hand-eye variety, it was at least ten minutes before I scored my first basket.

'She shoots, she scores!'

I high-fived my hottest imaginary teammate (Canball Xtreme is of course a mixed sport), cheerleadered over to the wastepaper basket and stooped down to retrieve my Coke can.

And that's when I spotted it.

Peeping out from a scrunched-up ball of paper was a face; a face I thought I recognised. It was the spitting image of that bloke in reception with the terrible acne and a dragon tattoo crawling up his neck. It must have been him because when I smoothed out the paper there were cartoons of that woman with the eyebrows in Starbucks, the intern guy with the crooked nose, and a nice one of Brian Simkins sitting on the photocopier with a bubble coming out of his mouth saying, 'Does my bum look big on this?'

Scrawled across the bottom of the page in black felt tip were seven random letters.

todtnau

What was that all about? I must have been pretty bored because I started trying to turn them into a well-known phrase or saying, like on that TV show Grandma watches. But the best I could come up with was DAN U TOT (totally odious turn-off?), so I tried saying it loud (TODD *NOW*!), in case it was a joke or something.

If it was, I didn't get it. And anyway, they hardly needed a caption; those pictures spoke for themselves. And I was grinning inanely when the door crashed open and someone started shouting at me.

'What the hell do you think you're doing in my office?' Unlike your average St Thomas's form tutor he was definitely angry, not just disappointed.

'I was . . .' Words failed me, but I had the presence of mind to stuff the piece of paper into my *Where's Wally?* sports bag before turning to face my accuser.

'I'm waiting,' he said. That *did* sound a bit like a St Thomas's teacher. 'You'd better have a good explanation or I'm going straight to security.' It was the same Steve who'd run away from me in Dad's office. Only this time he didn't look the slightest bit cute.

'Brian Simkins told me to wait for you,' I said.

'Old Sicknote?' said Steve, his twitching temples starting to recover. 'What for?'

'I'm on work experience. Brian said you were expecting me.'

'Oh yeah. Right,' said Steve, reclaiming the black swivel chair and slumping down at his workstation. 'I remember now. Sorry about that.'

'Forget it.'

He reached for his half-eaten cheeseburger. 'No need to look so disgusted. I never have time for a decent lunchbreak. Why do you want to do work experience in a dump like this?'

'Don't you like it here?'

'What do *you* think?' he said, forcing down a final mouthful of cold, reconstituted cow.

I was starting to warm to his rebel-without-a-cause act. 'Why do it then?'

'For the money, of course. What else?' said Steve. 'Believe it or not, I wanted to go to art college.'

'Money isn't everything,' I said, semi-repeating what Mr Catchpole told us when a show of hands revealed that at least half the PSHE class wanted to be overpaid celebrities.

'Try telling Chelsey that,' said Steve.

'Who's Chelsey?'

He glanced up at the fake-tanned figure in the photograph. 'My fiancée; she won't get her dream wedding if I don't . . .' He can't have been that much older than I was, but he'd already perfected that world-on-your-shoulders look that you only see in adults. 'DJs and canapés don't come cheap, you know.'

Dad had this theory that the longer couples obsessed about their wedding, the shorter the marriage was likely to last, but

I wasn't about to share relationship advice from a man in couples' therapy himself. So I lied through my teeth. 'She looks . . . a really good laugh.'

'Yes,' said Steve gloomily. 'Anyway, why did Sicknote send you down here?'

'He said something about explaining how the firewall works.'

Maybe it was just a bad day at the office. Steve still looked kind of adorable when he laughed. 'I think we can do better than that. Have you heard that remix of "Old Yellow Bricks" on YouTube?'

'Are you allowed to look at that sort of stuff at work?'

He winked and fired up his computer. 'If anyone asks, you can tell them we were checking out the firewall. Anyway, I won't tell if you don't.'

Steve had great taste in music; pity that Chelsey's was so 'totally lamestream'. He played me the five tracks he'd take to a desert island, and I showed him my favourite fail video of that nun falling out of a tree.

It was the fastest forty-five minutes of the week. And when Brian Simkins arrived, the weight of the world pressing down on his dandruff-flecked shoulders, I almost wished it wasn't my last day.

'So sorry I'm late,' he said. 'I hope I haven't inconvenienced you, Steven.'

'No problemo,' said Steve, his computer screen swiftly flicking from Nirvana live at The Paramount, to a row of incomprehensible digits. 'Jess here's a quick learner.'

Brian nodded and stepped carefully over the wastepaper basket. 'Yes, well, be seeing you.'

'Thanks a lot for showing me the firewall,' I said with a huge metaphorical wink. 'Oh, and good luck with the wedding.'

Steve was already tapping dejectedly at his keyboard by the time I'd squeezed into my court shoes and stumbled towards the lift.

'The meeting didn't go terribly well, I'm afraid,' said Brian, pushing the button for Reprographics. 'Still, your father's an extremely experienced professional. I'm sure he knows what he's doing.' He clicked his tongue infuriatingly. 'I just hope he realises what he's up against. The press could have a bloody field day.'

That's what gave me my first inkling that things were getting serious. It was the only time I'd ever heard Brian swear.

Angry Birds

It was the end of the day. Dad was late as usual, so I sat in reception with the beginnings of a headache, and only my phone for company. After I'd checked Facebook, launched a whole flock of angry birds and finished tweeting (*What sucks worse than Year Ten enrichment day? Work experience!!*), there was nothing for it but to read Dan Lulham's latest batch of texts. Same old, same old, and they were starting to get to me.

Jess n Dan. 2gether 4ever

It must have been nearly eight o'clock by the time Brian Simkins arrived with his top shirt button undone – a global calamity by his standards. 'I'm afraid your father's going to be working late. We've got a conference call with Moscow booked. But don't worry, there's a cab waiting to take you to the station.'

'Right. Fine.'

'This is my e-mail address. Now I know I haven't been as thorough as I might have been, so if there's ever anything I can do for you, please don't hesitate to get in touch.'

'Thanks, Brian,' I said, stuffing the white index card into the bowels of my *Where's Wally?* sports bag and trying desperately not to laugh.

Somewhere between East Croydon and Gatwick Airport I had an epiphany. You know, a eureka moment, like that guy in the bath? Maybe it was the woman opposite with the joyless tone in her voice as she duty-called her significant other with the earth shattering news she was 'on the train', or the haunted look that possessed Steve every time he mentioned Chelsey's dream wedding. Anyway, whatever it was, the thought of another long-term relationship was about as appealing as that problem-solving workshop we did on enrichment day. Six more weeks with a muppet like Dan Lulham was the last thing I needed – or anyone else for that matter. I didn't even read his final message, just fired off my most sensible text of the month.

no chance u 2 timing loser. I'm just not that desperate, Dan.

He probably wouldn't appreciate my ironic use of text-speak. It made *me* smile anyway. And I was feeling much better until I walked into the lounge and found Mum and the Golden One having one of their girly chats. I could just hear Mum telling the other 'fat ladies' at her aqua-aerobics coven that she and Millie were 'more like best friends than mother and daughter' – and it hurt.

'Hi, Jess,' said the Golden One, aka Amelia Emmeline

Hudson, aka my disgustingly perfect older sister. 'How was work experience?'

'All right,' I muttered, crash landing in my favourite spot on the sofa and reaching for the remote. 'Dad says he's going to be late.'

'Yes, we know,' said Mum tetchily. 'Pity he couldn't have called two hours ago.'

'He only found out at the last minute,' I said, doing my best to defend him. 'He's having a really hard time at work.'

Mum nearly choked on her marinated olive. 'And I'm not, I suppose. He wants to try working for the health service before he starts bleating on about his heavy schedule. If he thinks he can —'

'There's that celebrity hairdressing show in a minute,' said Millie, jumping in before Mum could go off on one. 'Why don't we all watch that?'

'Good idea, Mills,' said Mum. 'Let's hope that irritating woman from the Shopping Channel gets evicted.'

What can I tell you about the Golden One? Unlike most of the geeks at St Thomas's, she was smart enough *and* pretty enough to make the front page of the *County Times* on GCSE results day. And even though she'd been wowing her tutors at sixth form college for the past nine months, it didn't stop Mrs Mendoza reminding me that 'Millie picked up quadratic equations in about two seconds' or old Catchpole finding it 'almost inconceivable' that we'd emerged from the same gene pool.

She was just so perfect. Every time I screwed up (spoiler alert: big one coming up!), the gulf between us looked even wider. She'd even cut back on her social life to concentrate on getting into Oxford. How did that make me look when I rolled in from one of Ella's parties looking 'tired and emotional'? How could I ever compete with the mind of Steven Hawking and the body of a supermodel?

Halfway through the beach-hair photo shoot, Mum's phone went off. It was mildly amusing when she first got it, but her 'Staying Alive' ringtone was starting to do my head in. 'Oh well, that's just great . . . You can't keep doing this, you know . . .'

It was obvious who was calling from the angry policeman in her voice.

'You see, this is exactly what Tricia's talking about . . . I don't care if your bloody job *is* on the line. Try thinking about your marriage for once . . . Forget it . . . No, look, just forget it, OK?'

Mum grabbed the newspaper, launching herself off the sofa like an angry bride. 'That was your father. Surprise, surprise, they're having another meeting, so he's staying in town tonight. Anyway, I'm off to bed.'

'I thought you wanted to see Justine's highlights,' I said.

'Not in the mood,' said Mum, shuffling across to the door. 'Turn the lights out when you come up, won't you?'

I zapped a footballer's wife with the remote. Even a *celebrity* hairdresser ought to know the difference between loose curls and ringlets.

We sat in silence for a bit – just like Mum and Dad on Sunday afternoons. I don't know what Millie was thinking, but I was half wondering where we'd be spending Christmas.

'Don't worry,' she said, her toothpaste-advert smile already starting to work its magic. 'They'll come through this, I promise.'

I wondered if she knew about their counselling sessions. But of course she did. Mum told the Golden One everything. She was just so capable, so comfortable in her own – meticulously exfoliated – skin. Whatever crap you threw at my sister, she always came up smelling of roses. At least, that's what I thought then.

But I'm getting ahead of myself. Before I do anything else, I should probably tell you what happened halfway through the last lesson on the following Monday afternoon. If I could skip over it, believe me, I would. The trouble is, it kind of explains how I acted later. That doesn't mean it isn't still painful though. 'Personal tragedy' doesn't even come close.

Everyone
Get the Picture?

'Are you Mr Colin Catchpole?'

'That's right, Officer. How may I help you?'

'I'm afraid I've got some *really* bad news for you, sir. It's your fifteen-year-old daughter, sir. She's dead.'

Mr Catchpole stared out at the all-weather hockey pitches and sniffed up a gobbet of snot. 'I'm sorry, Officer. I don't understand.'

'Well, you know, sir. Not living? Snuffed it?'

'But that's impossible. Gillian was always so healthy. Isn't that right, Mrs Catchpole?'

'What? Oh yeah, yeah. She was well fit. Sorry. Sorry, I'm not laughing, *Colin*. It's just a bit of a shock.'

I don't want to disappoint anyone, but this is not another

story about a dying teenager. Millie used to love all that. Anything with a terminal illness and an unhappy, but ultimately life-affirming ending and she was hooked. No, it was just one of Mr Catchpole's role-playing exercises. How was it that St Thomas's 'favourite' PSHE teacher/war graves guru, managed to turn all the exciting stuff (sex, drugs, bacon rolls) into something about as gripping as an arthritic granny?

'But how did it happen?' said Mr Catchpole, fixing his 'wife' with a grief stricken glare. 'She was fine on the way to the party.'

The Year Ten wise guys offered up a few helpful suggestions.

'Probably binge drinking.'

'Was she being bullied, sir?'

'Or dangerous driving. You know what young people are like when they get behind the wheel.'

'Was it an accident in the workplace?'

'How about too much junk food?'

Mr Catchpole stepped, diva-like, out of character. 'Look, this is *not* a pantomime.'

'Oh yes it is.'

'And *I'll* have that, thank you, Aidan,' he bellowed, his upturned palm extended in front of him until Aidan Corcoran emerged from his metal-head coma and handed over his iPod. 'It wouldn't be so bad if you were listening to something decent. No doubt it's another tuneless cacophony with sub-adolescent lyrics and a throbbing baseline.'

Aidan Corcoran made no attempt to defend his taste in music.

'Well, you can see me afterwards,' said Mr Catchpole. 'Now, where was I?'

'Your daughter, sir. She's dead.'

Considering we'd spent the first twenty minutes brushing up on the street names of every drug from aerosols to XTC, we hardly needed the cast of *CSI: Miami* to establish the cause of death. So while Mr Catchpole conducted a post-mortem, *I* tried to establish the cause of the buzz of excitement that had suddenly circled the temporary classroom.

It happened all the time at St Thomas's. Someone's mobile went off in the middle of a lesson and the next thing you knew, every kid's in the class was vibrating. Ninety-eight per cent of the rumours that went round were just some saddo with a score to settle. Put it this way, we'd had about twenty 'teenage pregnancies' since Christmas, but unless half of them turned out to be virgin births and Darren Denyer really *had* had a sex change, by my calculations only about 0.4 of them would be pushing a screaming brat round Sainsbury's next year.

Even so, I had high hopes for this one. There'd been nothing juicy on Two-Faced Book since that thing about Shezza Morgan's boob job, but by the way Izzy and Tania were cackling into their hidden mobiles, this was obviously right up there with Rob the Slob's prom date.

'Let's have a look,' I whispered to the boy in front, whose name I could never remember. 'Oh come on, don't be an idiot. I'd show you mine.'

'Yeah, I bet you would,' he said, his creepy smile making me even more glad I'd made zero effort to get to know him.

I couldn't believe no one had sent *me* anything. And then I realised why.

Ella tapped me on the shoulder and handed me her phone. 'You'd better have a look at this, babes.'

Shock competed with anger, and anger won. No wonder they were all wetting themselves.

That photo was supposed to be *private*. How could I ever show my face in public now that the whole school had had a glimpse of so much more?

'I've seen worse,' said Ella, handing me a tissue. 'It's actually quite tasteful, babes. Don't worry, they'll all have forgotten by next week.'

'Are you kidding?'

Thank God old Catchpole had arrived at his learning objective. 'Right, perhaps someone would like to tell me what they've gleaned from today's lesson?'

'That Ella's rubbish at acting?'

'That the drugs don't work?'

But it was the last suggestion that got the biggest laugh.

'That you should always be careful who you share your photos with?'

Mr Catchpole was stuffing his visual aids into a Tesco bag. 'Yes, well, I'm glad you were listening *last* week, Damien, but I fail to see what that's got to do with —'

The bell went, and I was out of that door faster than a celebrity mum gets back to size zero after a difficult birth. There was no way I'd be sticking around for the inevitable five-day festival of smartarse commentary. And Ella's brand of glee and sympathy was even worse.

Rampant with rage, I shot past the *Keep Calm and Carry On* poster in the corridor, adrenalin pumping. I knew exactly who'd done it, and I knew exactly where to find him. If he wanted a fight, that was exactly what he was going to get.

A Neanderthal 'Whoooooaaa' went up when they spotted

me approaching the bus stop.

I pressed my fingernails into the palm of my hands, already wishing that I'd stopped to retouch my mascara.

'Sorry, Jess,' said one of his dumb mates. 'We didn't recognise you with all your clothes on!'

'Well, you must be going blind, then. And we all know why that is.'

If Dan Lulham was feeling guilty, he certainly didn't show it. He was standing in the bus shelter with a disgustingly slippery smile on his face. 'All right, Jess?'

'What do *you* think?'

He shrugged and went back to checking his mobile.

'Why did you do it?' I shouted. 'That photo was supposed to be private. You swore you'd never show it to anyone.'

'Yeah, and you swore we'd be friends forever, so how come you dumped me?'

'Because you had your tongue in Natalie Corcoran's big mouth, that's why.'

'I told you about that. I was just —'

'You said you wanted it to remind you how . . . how . . . how beautiful I was. Not so you could send it to your pathetic mates.'

His pathetic mates sniggered.

'And you actually believed me?' said Dan. 'Get over yourself, *Jessica*.'

'You sent about a million texts begging me to go out with you again.'

The school bus pulled into the parking bay. The doors opened and Dan Lulham raced up the steps. 'Yes and I was right, wasn't I?' he said. 'I told you I'd get you back.'

My first instinct was to run up the stairs after him and stick my fingers in his eyes. But as soon as Barry the bus driver started his stupid 'no spitting, kicking, biting or eye-gouging' routine, I realised the journey would be a nightmare. How could I ever get the bus again? How could I ever walk into assembly with my head held high?

'What's the matter?' said Dan Lulham. 'Won't the supermodel be joining us today? That's a shame, because some of your new fans are just dying to meet you.'

I didn't want him to see me crying, so I shouted a whole load of stuff that Mr Catchpole would have called the sign of an 'impoverished vocabulary' before hitting him with the one insult that I knew would really hurt. 'Your hair looks crap by the way.'

It took me an hour to walk home. Every time a car with a St Thomas's kid went past, I slunk further into the shadows, like a vampire at dawn.

There was one good thing anyway: afternoon surgery must have finished early because Mum's black Volvo was parked in the drive. It almost set me off again – and according to Dad, it was only men who got emotional about cars.

Relief beckoned as I twisted my key in the lock. Home was the one place in the world I really felt safe. No matter what happened on the outside, things always looked a whole lot better the moment I walked into the house.

All that was about to change.

Things
Get Worse

I knew something was wrong when I heard them shouting. Mum was no stranger to the rising decibel, but the last time the Golden One had gone off on one like that she was still fastening her shoes with Velcro.

I stood in the hallway, wondering how 'best friends' had suddenly turned into mother and estranged ('she's pregnant by her stepfather's boyfriend') daughter on American daytime telly.

The kitchen door was shut. All I could make out was the occasional word or two, bubbling up from a cauldron of hostility.

'*Gurglegurglegurgle* UNBELIEVABLE *gurglegurgle* OUGHT TO BE . . . *gurglegurgle* OF ALL THE BLOODY . . .

gurglegurgle . . . GOT TO TELL HER, MUM *gurglegurgle* WHY WOULD ANYONE DO SOMETHING LIKE . . . *gurglegurgle* . . .'

The kitchen went silent as I pushed open the door. All I could hear was the faint hum of the dishwasher, and Mum's face forcing itself into a smile. 'Hi, Jess, how was —?'

'What's going on?' I said.

Millie didn't need to wear much make-up. At least, that's what they were always telling *me*. But it was obvious from the 'tasteful' streaks of mascara that she'd been crying. 'There's something you need to know about, Jess.'

Mum aimed her anti-bacterial spray at the chopping board, carefully avoiding eye contact as she turned to face me. 'You'd better sit down.'

It was what they said in soaps when they wanted to break bad news. I preferred standing for it, like the national anthem. 'What is it? Just *tell* me, Mum, you're scaring me now.'

'It's your father,' she said.

My heart did whatever hearts do when the one thing you fear most jumps out in front of you and screams. 'What's the matter with him? He's not . . . ?'

'*No*,' said Mum, declaring all out germ warfare on the work surfaces. 'It's not that, it's —'

'He's not had a heart attack, has he? I knew he was stressed out but —'

'He's *not* had a bloody heart attack,' said Mum. Having successfully slaughtered ninety-nine per cent of all known living germs, she was attacking the toaster in search of the elusive, final one per cent. 'There's nothing wrong with him. Not like that anyway.'

'Stop it,' I said. 'Just tell me what's happened to him.'

Mum dropped her weapon, the fight draining out of her, like a convict with nowhere left to run. 'He's been suspended from work, Jess. Gross misconduct. I'm afraid he won't be —'

'I knew it,' I said, relieved that it wasn't life-threatening, but at the same time furious on Dad's behalf. 'I *knew* there was something dodgy going on.'

Mum's face went white. 'How could you have done?'

'She couldn't,' said Millie emphatically. 'Could you, Jess?'

'It's something to do with that Russian thing, isn't it? Dad never talked to me about it, but I'm not blind, I could see how important it was.'

Mum looked lost. Not just lost for words, but like a toddler who can't find her mum in Sainsbury's.

And it was starting to make sense. 'Brian said it could all blow up in his face. Well, that's what's happened, isn't it? Something went wrong. And now Dad's got to take the blame. I'm right, aren't I?'

The dishwasher was first to break the silence, beeping six times before Mum finally whispered, 'Yes. Yes, that's right, Jess. Something like that.'

'*Mum*,' said Millie. 'What about —?'

'That's *enough*, Amelia,' said Mum. 'This is difficult enough without you sticking your nose in every five seconds. We'll discuss it later, when we've all calmed down.'

'Why can't we discuss it now?' I said.

'Because I say so,' said Mum, smashing her fist down on the draining board. 'Look, as soon as I find out something more . . . concrete, you two will be the first to know.'

Millie slung her leather messenger bag across her shoulder and marched to the door. 'Well, I hope you know what you're doing.'

'Not really,' said Mum, tearfully. 'I'm just trying to do what's best for all of us.'

'What's the matter with *her*?' I said, noting the unfamiliar sound of Millie's bedroom door slamming shut.

'She's upset. About your father. I'll go up and have a little chat with her while you're getting changed.'

Talk about role reversal. *I* was supposed to be the door slammer of the family. 'Don't worry, Mum. I'm sure she'll be fine when Dad gets home.'

Mum didn't say anything; she just ripped a handful of fresh basil from the pot on the windowsill and reached for a saucepan.

Mum's little chat had obviously failed epically. The lounge was simmering with unspoken resentment when Millie finally joined us for tea. We sat on the sofa, picking at our prawn and tomato pasta, the comforting murmur of the television relieving us from the burden of conversation. Dad's favourite celebrity chef was somehow managing to make bread and butter pudding look sexy. Mum normally spent half the programme heckling ('Apparently you need to get your cleavage out or the dough won't rise'), but her mind was obviously elsewhere.

It took me years to perfect my sulky teenager act. Millie seemed to have picked it up in half an hour. And why was Mum so angry? Surely it was time to forget their differences and show some support for Dad.

'Hey, Mum, Dad would really like that pudding, wouldn't he?' I said, hoping she'd come out with one of her caustic comments about the chef's yo-yo dieting.

'Would he?'

'You know he would.'

But Dad's taste in stodgy puddings was far from the only thing on my mind. I was worried sick about that photograph. The very thought of walking into my tutor base the next morning was giving me stomach cramps. It would be just like that lot to beam it onto every interactive whiteboard at St Thomas's. And it would be all over Facebook by now. Ella was probably texting me every five seconds with an update ('Sorry, babes, you've gone viral'), so it was just as well I'd switched my phone off and hidden it in my sports bag. Pity Mum hadn't done the same thing. Her ridiculous ringtone shattered the uneasy silence, like an ice-cream van at a funeral.

'Who is this, please?' said Mum, dumping her pasta bowl on the coffee table and rising slowly from the sofa. 'And how did you get my number?'

Millie reached for the remote, putting Dad's favourite chef on mute (which probably wouldn't have bothered him that much) so she could listen to Mum's phonecall and finish desecrating her once perfect fingernails.

'Well, I don't want to talk to *you*,' said Mum, pacing between the bookcase and that photo of the whole family screaming delightedly on the log-flume ride at Legoland. 'Where did you get your information from, anyway? It's supposed to be confidential . . . Public interest? Do me a favour.' She stared at the faded photograph, probably wishing that Mr Lego had invented a time-machine. 'No comment . . . No comment. Look, I don't have to put up with this, you know. Don't ever call me or anyone in my family again. *Good night*.'

Five seconds later, her phone started ringing again. And again and again until she turned it off completely, which was practically unheard of.

'Who was it?' I said. 'And why have you turned your phone off?'

'It was a journalist,' said Mum. 'She wanted to know about your father.'

'But why?' I said. 'I mean, who cares? It's not like Dad's a celebrity or something. People get suspended from work every day.'

'Yes but . . .' Mum reminded me of the boy who forgot his lines in Millie's drama presentation. Mum stood there with a look of pure panic on her face, scanning the room for a prompter.

And it was Millie who came to the rescue, just like she did in the play. 'You know what it's like, Jess. Bankers aren't exactly flavour of the month these days. The media loves a juicy banking scandal.'

'Brian told me the press could have a field day,' I said, 'but I thought he was just exaggerating. That bloke thinks mergers and acquisitions should have their own movie deal.'

'Well, there you are, then,' said Mum.

And then the landline went. Millie raced out to the hall and started screaming down the receiver, with 'Scum of the earth' being the only phrase that might just have made it onto children's TV. She sounded more like a character from the play than the Golden One. (Dad said if he'd come out with some random swearing no one would have guessed the boy with the 'unfortunate haircut' had forgotten his lines.)

'Yeah, and I hope your children are really proud of you,' said

37

Millie, sweeping the phone and Dad's tin of dead biros onto the hall carpet, before stumbling back into the lounge and throwing herself at Mum. 'How can they do this to us? *We* haven't done anything wrong.'

'No,' I said, unmuting and switching to a documentary about a girl who could only eat tomato soup. 'And neither has Dad.'

Mum froze for a moment before wrapping her arms around Millie and gently stroking her long black hair.

The girl in the documentary was taking her first tentative steps with solids when someone started banging on the front door. But it wasn't one of those chirpy, 'We can save you money on your gas bill' type of knocks. It sounded ominous, like the prelude to bad news.

'I'll get it,' said Millie.

'I'm coming with you,' said Mum.

All three of us crept out to the front door and looked up at the shady figure behind the frosted glass.

'Who is it?' shouted Mum.

'Are you Mrs Margaret Hudson?' growled the voice.

'*Doctor* Margaret Hudson.'

'Even better,' said the voice. 'Look, I just want to ask you a few questions – that's all. Can I come in please?'

'It's another journalist,' whispered Millie. 'Tell him to get lost.'

'We're busy,' said Mum.

'That's all right,' said the voice. 'I'll wait.'

'I've got nothing to say to you,' said Mum.

'How about a quick photo, then?'

Mum was perilously close to losing it completely. 'What is

the matter with you people? Can't any of you take no for an answer? It's nothing to do with us anyway.'

'Exactly,' said the voice of reason. 'That's why I'm sure you'd appreciate the chance to put your side of the story across.'

'Look, if you don't get off my property in the next two minutes, I'll call the police,' said Mum.

'All right then, *Doctor*,' said the voice. 'I'll wait in the street. Let's hope the neighbours don't start asking questions.'

Millie screamed some more lines from that play, the gist of which was that he should do something physically impossible with his camera and return to the gutter from whence he came.

The voice sounded unimpressed. 'I'm not going anywhere. Not until you decide to cooperate. Look, I probably shouldn't tell you this, Margaret, but if *you* don't say anything, I'll have to make it up.'

'Go to hell!' roared Mum.

The girl in the documentary was wolfing down an enormous cheeseburger; the guy with the camera was still camped out at the bottom of our drive. We watched him through a chink in the curtains as he checked his BlackBerry in the yellowy glow of the streetlights.

'Right, that's it,' said Mum. 'I'm not putting up with this for the next God knows how long.'

'What do you mean?' said Millie.

'We're getting out of here. I will not be held prisoner in my own house.'

'We can't just take off in the middle of the night,' I said.

'Don't worry,' said Mum. 'I had a terrible feeling the press might come sniffing around, so I packed a suitcase for all of us

39

and chucked it in the back of the car.'

'Where would we go anyway?' said Millie.

'It's OK, I've thought of that too. Now, if you two want any bits and bobs, you'd better run upstairs and fetch them. I'll give you five minutes.'

'But what about work?' I said. 'Doctors aren't allowed to throw sickies. You told me that yourself.'

'There are plenty of locums out there, Jess. I'll call the surgery in the morning. *Please* don't make this any harder than it has to be. The sooner we get on the road, the sooner we get there.'

I had an idea she was talking about that health spa she went to with the bipolar radiographer from work, which would have been fine by me if it wasn't for one crucial detail. 'And what about Dad? It's not fair on him. How's he going to feel when he walks in here tonight and we've abandoned him? *Tell* her, Millie.'

The Golden One flashed me the sort of smile that Mum perfected at medical school for breaking bad news to the relatives. 'Dad's not coming home tonight, Jess. He's driving down to Grandma's. He's going to stay there until —'

'I want to talk to him,' I said. 'I'm not going anywhere until I know he's OK with this.'

'Sorry, my love,' said Mum. 'He'll have turned his phone off. Well, you've seen what it's like. It's probably best if we *all* keep a low profile for a bit.'

'Best for who?' I said.

'Look, we haven't got time for this,' said Mum. 'If there's anything you think you might need, go and get it – *now*.'

'Well, how long are we going for?' I said. 'A couple of days? A week?'

'I don't know,' said Mum. 'As long as it takes. Now, for God's sake get a move on, Jess. We're leaving in ten minutes.'

'Well, all right,' I said, 'but you'd better have remembered my strappy black top.'

I sometimes wonder if I should have stood my ground – locked myself in my bedroom (I'd done that a few times) and refused to come out. But Mum seemed so sure about it, so certain it was the right thing to do. And as far as I could tell, the Golden One felt the same way. But that wasn't the real reason I raced upstairs without complaining and started shaking school books out of my *Where's Wally?* bag. The real reason was a bit more selfish. It was that photo.

As Brian Simkins never tired of saying, Dad was probably the most talented analyst he'd ever worked with. He was also the most honest man in the universe, so I was totally confident Dad would sort things out in the end. What I wasn't so confident about was my own ability to make it through school the next morning without ending up in therapy. It sounds pathetic, I know, but I just couldn't face Dan Lulham's smug 'I told you so's or the Year Ten haters laughing at me behind my back. A few days at a health spa was just what the doctor ordered.

So I did what Mum said: tossed the bare essentials into my *Where's Wally?* sports bag. Phone and iPod (they were in there already), half a packet of Juicy Fruit and some sanitary towels. Plus a few basic cosmetics, of course: two types of shampoo and conditioner, anti-frizz serum, foundation, mascara, eye-liner, hair mask, face mask, cleanser, toner, hair-straighteners, hair dryer, round brush, regular brush, hairbands, hair clips, nail varnish (top coat, bottom coat, three colours and some

41

remover), perfume, deodorant and a packet of wipes.

I couldn't resist one luxury item. Even if it was only for a couple of days, I knew how much I'd miss him. And I wasn't exactly proud of myself for running out on him like that. So I squeezed in a photo of Dad (that one when we'd just tipped a bucket of cold water over him in the paddling pool) and ran downstairs.

'Right,' said Mum. 'Have you both switched your lights off?'

After I'd come down again, Mum gave us our final instructions. It was the first and probably final time we'd ever see her with the hood of her Marks & Spencer's hoodie up. 'OK, when I give the signal, we need to get to that car as quickly as possible. And keep your faces covered. We don't want him getting any photographs.'

It reminded me of Mr Catchpole's speech in the trenches about what it must have felt like the moment before you went over the top. I shivered in the darkness, wondering how anyone in their right mind would exchange such a cosy existence for a life on the run, trying to convince myself it would all be over by Christmas.

'Are you sure about this?' said Millie.

'Yes,' said Mum, reaching for the handle and pushing open the front door. 'OK, girls, let's go go go!'

Mum aimed her keyring at the black Volvo in the drive. It blinked back at us as the locks clicked open, and we scrunched towards it across the gravel.

I chucked my sports bag onto the back seat and jumped in.

The man with the camera leaped onto the driveway, barring our exit with his arms outstretched.

Mum didn't even ask us if we'd put on our seatbelts. She just stamped down on the accelerator and drove straight at him.

The man with the camera threw himself sideways into the hedge, somehow managing to press his lens up against the car window and flash at us as we screeched past.

It ought to have been exhilarating, like something from those bank job movies that Dad only dared put on if Mum was out clothes shopping. And it *almost* was, until Millie turned round and fixed me with the kind of smile reserved only for the evictees of TV talent shows or the terminally ill. 'You OK, Jess?'

I nodded mechanically, but inside it had suddenly hit home. A few days off school were an easy sell to the likes of me. And Mum wasn't exactly immune to the odd bout of irrational behaviour. But despite the fact that the exams were over and, according to her, most of the teachers were already mentally sunning themselves on a beach somewhere, for Millie to miss a single hour of sixth form college was a *really* big deal.

That's when I realised how serious it was.

Pee Break

According to Google, it should have taken approximately nine hours and forty-five minutes, not allowing for the midnight pee break and an unscheduled tour of Coventry courtesy of Sally Sat-Nav.

But you don't want to hear about the journey – Mum driving like a lunatic, Millie gradually retreating into a silent world of her own, and me watching classic, epic fail videos on my iPod (the car in the river, the curious incident of the rabbit in the swimming pool, the exploding biscuit tin, the bald fat bloke falling off a table and that one of the birthday cake setting fire to the curtains and all the kids going mental).

Somewhere between Crewe and Manchester, epic fail videos morphed into epic fail nightmares: Mum and Dad walking down the aisle on their wedding day and the church bursting into flames, Millie opening her exam results for that guy with the camera and pulling out a big fat *FAIL*, and the Demon Headmaster announcing in assembly that 'the much debated photograph of Jessica Hudson will be on display in the learning resources centre as a permanent reminder of her crass stupidity'.

My relief at waking vanished the moment I remembered where I was. Not snuggling peacefully beneath my duck feather duvet while Mum screamed 'Get a bloody move on, Jessica,' from the bottom of the stairs, but belted into the back seat of a Volvo with a super-sized crick in my neck and a pounding headache. And when I peered out of the rain-spattered window, it started feeling like one of those nightmares within a nightmare that you get in horror movies. High above me, a rocky peak was disappearing into the clouds. That trip to the health spa was looking distinctly unlikely.

'Where are we?' I said.

'Bonny Scotland,' said Mum, sounding a whole a lot calmer than the night before. 'We've been driving all night.'

'So what happened to all that "never drive when you're tired" stuff? You must be exhausted.'

'I'm fine.'

'And what are we doing in Scotland? You never said anything about Scotland.'

'I'll tell you when we stop,' said Mum. 'I want to explain properly.'

The inside of my mouth felt like a sandpaper factory in the Sahara desert. 'Can we get something to eat? I'm really hungry.'

'Well, you're in luck,' said Mum. 'According to Sally Sat-Nav,

45

this is the last service station for the next hundred miles. What about you, Millie? Fancy some breakfast?'

Millie grunted and turned up the volume on her iPod.

I love service stations. The smell of fast food, a satisfying trip to a 'regularly inspected' lavatory, disposable toothbrushes, little kids on arcade game killing sprees, fruit machines flashing enticingly and the feeling that everyone is on their way to a better place – except us, of course.

'You still haven't told us where we're going,' I said, biting into my stale doughnut.

Mum poured three sachets of sugar into her cappuccino and glanced anxiously at the rolling news channel on the giant screen above. 'You remember my friend Sue?'

'What, Sue the nutter?' I said.

'She's not a nutter, Jess,' said Mum, smiling. 'She's just eccentric, that's all.'

Sue was Mum's best friend at university. In fact, she went out with Dad a few times before deciding that he and Mum were 'a match made in heaven' and setting them up on a blind date. On the face of it, Mum and Sue didn't have much in common (Sue was arty, and according to Dad she'd never had a 'proper' job or a 'proper' relationship in her life), but they'd managed to stay in touch long before Facebook turned friendship into an Olympic competition. Every couple of years or so, Sue would turn up at our house with weird presents, like that wooden board game we never worked out how to play and the one-eyed glass dog that was supposed to ward off evil spirits.

'What about her, anyway?' I said, remembering how she'd tried to persuade Dad to have a go at 'rebirthing'.

Mum gulped down a mouthful of cappuccino. 'Well, you remember that YouTube video I showed you?'

Millie sussed it out way before I did. 'Oh no. No, no, *no*. No, Mum, NO. Absolutely no way.'

'Hang on a minute,' said Mum. 'Let me explain.'

'Don't bother,' said Millie. 'I'm *not* spending the next six weeks with a bunch of tree-hugging weirdos.'

'They're conservationists,' said Mum. 'What's weird about that?'

I suddenly realised what she was getting at. 'You're not seriously thinking about taking us *there*, are you? You said you'd rather go fly fishing with Jeremy Clarkson than live without a hot bath. And what's all this about six weeks?'

'Sue wrote to me a couple of months back,' said Mum. 'Their doctor had left suddenly, and she asked if I'd consider helping out for the summer holidays. Of course, your father was having none of it, so I didn't give it another thought. But now —'

'Mum, we *can't*,' I said. 'Dad will think we're abandoning him. And you saw their video. It was horrible! That lot – what do they call themselves again?'

'The Dawdlers,' said Mum.

I knew it was something ridiculous. 'Yeah, well that says it all, doesn't it? Think about it. Living with them would be like going back to the Dark Ages. And anyway, according to you, Sue was never going to stick it out for longer than a month.'

'Well, she has,' said Mum. 'They must be getting desperate because I had another letter last week.'

'I still don't see why they've got a YouTube video in the first place,' said Millie. 'I thought the whole point was that they didn't use any technology.

'They don't,' said Mum. 'That's why it's so perfect.'

'How do you work that one out?' said Millie.

'Think about it,' said Mum. 'No internet, no television. No phones, no newspapers.'

'And no photographers,' added Millie.

'That's right,' said Mum. 'It's about the only place on earth we can get away from it all.'

I couldn't believe it. She'd laughed louder than anyone when we'd watched their leader guy doing a big speech about how the worldwide web had 'enslaved humanity', and how a life without microwaves and satellite telly was the only answer. But now she was making out it was the best idea since peel-off nail varnish.

'Why can't we just go to a hotel or something?' I asked. 'This stuff with Dad, people are going to forget about it in two minutes. We don't need to run off to some stupid island. Tell her, Millie.'

The Golden One was checking out the rolling news channel too. 'Maybe Mum's right. Maybe it's for the best.'

She'd certainly changed her tune. But what could I do? I was miles away from anywhere and at least three years from my first major credit card. 'Then we have to tell Dad where we're going.'

'*No*,' said Mum. 'He's got his phone turned off anyway. I'll write to him. I think there's a mail boat or something. You never know, Jess, you might even enjoy it.'

'Look, Mum, you can drag me off to the middle of nowhere, but please don't insult my intelligence, OK?'

'You'd better pop to the loo again,' said Mum. 'We've got fifty more miles to go yet.'

Who Pays
the Ferryman?

Sally Sat-Nav had already sent us to Coventry. Now Millie was
doing exactly the same thing. She hadn't said a word since the
service station. She'd just plugged in her headphones and
closed her eyes.

Not that there was anything to see, only mile after mile of
boring countryside. Snow-capped mountains through one
window, a craggy coastline out of the other. And not a single
shop in sight. I was starting to wonder if a few weeks of torture
at St Thomas's might not have been the easier option.

Sally Sat-Nav seemed to be having a nightmare too.
According to her, we'd finally reached our destination.

'That's strange,' said Mum, pulling up on the grass verge. 'It
looks completely deserted.'

All I could make out was a white wall of surf. 'This is stupid, Mum. Why don't we just go home?'

'I thought I'd explained all that,' said Mum. 'Now get your coats on. Sue was certainly right about the weather up here.'

Mum opened the door. An icy blast shot through the Volvo, instantly killing the suffocating warmth.

'Forget it,' said Millie. 'I'm staying here.'

'Fair enough. Looks like it's just you and me, Jess.'

I kind of liked that. It was *never* me and Mum. The only one-on-one time *we* ever got was when she popped upstairs for a little chat about my inability to make 'appropriate lifestyle choices' (lucky she hadn't heard about the photograph) and the necessity of taking my schoolwork more seriously before it was 'too late'.

'OK then,' I said, pulling on the disgustingly red and bulbous anorak that Mum had somehow believed was an appropriate fashion choice for school. I'd never worn it, of course, but the chances of running into another St Thomas's kid were just about unlikely enough to risk it.

'We'll be back in a minute, Millie,' said Mum. 'You can get our bags together while you're waiting.'

Whatever Millie muttered was partially censored by the wind, so Mum chose to ignore it. 'Come on,' she said. 'Let's see what we can find.'

It stank of dead fish, and the air was so thick with rain and seawater that it was like going through a car wash without your car. We stumbled across the slippery pebbles towards the deep-throated roar of the sea. My hair was . . . Sorry, I don't really want to talk about my hair right now. All I knew was that the moment we got there I'd be smothering it in anti-frizz serum.

'What's that?' said Mum, pointing into the distance, and upping her pace to a middle-aged jog.

'Mum, wait,' I said, struggling to keep up with her.

Down at the water's edge a small stone jetty jutted out into the sea. 'Now careful on these steps, Jess, they're really slippy.'

It was the first time since primary school I'd felt glad to have 'wrapped up warm'. A watery wall of death flew skywards every time a wave battered the jetty. Hood up and head down, I trailed Mum across the treacherous granite.

At the far end was a white noticeboard wearing a blue lifebelt. Pinned to the noticeboard was a fading piece of paper in a plastic wallet.

VISITORS TO THE ISLANDS
SOUND THE KLAXON THREE TIMES
AND WAIT FOR THE FERRY

'Go on,' said Mum, pointing at the red button. 'You do it.'

I hesitated for a moment, knowing once I'd pressed that thing there was no turning back. But like I said, I didn't have much choice. Plus, I kind of wanted to hear what noise it made.

Three immense blasts, like an enormous passenger ship coming into harbour or a choir of gifted and talented whales, echoed out across the bluey-green waters. The ferry was on its way.

'Right,' said Mum. 'Let's go get our things.'

Millie wanted to wait in the warm. Mum started off with gentle cajoling, moving swiftly on to the 'bad cop' act that she'd perfected on me. 'Look, I'm not going to ask you again, Amelia. Just do as I say or I'll have to . . .'

Millie flashed her a one-fingered salute.

'Sorry, Jess,' said Mum. 'I think your sister and I need a little chat.'

She walked round to the other side of the car and climbed into the driver's seat. The central locking clicked shut.

The windows had misted over, so I couldn't even study their body language, let alone hear what Mum was saying. But it must have been pretty persuasive, because three minutes later the Golden One emerged from the car clutching a brown holdall and my *Where's Wally?* sports bag.

'Here's your bag, Jess,' she whispered, the weather conditions making it impossible to decide if she was crying or just windswept.

Either way, she looked so miserable that for the first time in fifteen years it seemed like I was the one who should be looking after *her*. I'd been trying to convince myself that all Mum really wanted was some thinking time, that a short break from Dad was just what she needed to get their marriage back on track. Maybe I could convince my sister too. 'Don't worry, Mills. It'll be OK, I promise. They'll work things out, I know they will. And then we can all go home again.'

People had written songs about Millie's laugh. Well, that guy at college, anyway – the one in the band with a silly name (Salmon Fishing In Yemen) who had this massive crush on her. But the laugh she laughed now was nothing like a 'warm warm scarf' or even a 'hot hot bath' and it certainly didn't make you 'really really wanna get her autograph'. It was angry and bitter, with a touch of madness about it.

'We'd better get down to the jetty,' said Mum. 'We don't want to miss the damned thing.'

It kind of reminded me of the time we got stranded at Heathrow Airport – except that lasted three days, of course.

Mum sat on the suitcase with her head in her hands. Its tiny plastic wheels were pretty useful in an airport, but on a pebbly beach they were about as handy as hair straighteners at a convention of Buddhist monks.

Millie was blowing her head off with a bass-heavy ditty that sounded more like dubstep than her usual brand of indie whining.

I was concentrating on the horizon. The magazine Mum bought me at the service station was more saturated and out of control than my hair, so I'd given up on twenty ways to banish split ends and stood mesmerised by the slow rise and fall of the waves, desperate for anything that could break the tension.

Dad would have known what to do. He was brilliant at the airport, ferrying Mum and Millie a constant stream of skinny cappuccinos, me a year's supply of Tic-Tacs and gummy bears, and keeping us entertained with his impersonation of the indecipherable flight announcer.

No one else was going to make the effort. It was up to me to get the ball rolling. 'I don't think Dad would have parked on the grass like that.'

'Dad's not here, is he?' snapped Mum.

Thirty uncomfortable seconds later, I tried again. 'Did you know side plaits are making a comeback?'

'Really,' said Mum, gnawing hard on her bottom lip.

I'd given up by the time I spotted the small white boat in

the distance, riding the waves like a roller coaster. As it got closer, I saw that the ferryman was a bloke of about Dad's age, but with even less fashion sense (we're talking yellow cagoule with matching trousers here) and a disgustingly shiny bald head. Even so, I was almost as relieved as Mum when he started pulling up alongside the jetty.

'Thank God for that,' she said. 'Now remember, if he asks any questions, don't tell him your real names.'

After several attempts, the ferryman managed to wrap a rope around the big metal post on the side of the jetty and pull it tight. 'You rang, milady?'

Why did every bus driver and ferryman in the world think they were some kind of a comedian?

'Er, yes,' said Mum. 'We need to get to one of the islands.'

'Then you'd better step aboard, me hearties.'

He didn't sound very Scottish. He didn't sound much like a pirate either – more like Mr Catchpole's Captain Hook in that terrible staff pantomime.

'You two girls had better go first,' said Mum, already turning her traditional shade of green.

There was about a metre's drop into the boat. Millie stepped calmly off the side of the jetty, earphones still blazing, and made her way to a seat at the front. I'm not that great at heights, but with the help of the ferryman, I stumbled gracelessly to what I remembered from the Year Seven trip to the Lakeside activity centre was called amidships.

Mum stood nervously on the edge, like a young ostrich contemplating flight. 'Would you mind taking my suitcase? I'm not much of a sailor, I'm afraid.'

'That's all right,' said the ferryman. 'Neither am I. *Joke*,' he added, clocking how anxious she looked.

'Well, please don't,' said Mum, grabbing his hand and screwing her eyes tight shut.

The boat rocked alarmingly as he caught hold of her suitcase and then proceeded to catch hold of her. 'Steady, you'll have us all over. I don't know about you, but I always prefer to be in a swimming costume.'

'Sorry,' said Mum, lurching from side to side before regaining her balance and plonking herself down next to me. 'I'm sure I'll be fine once we get going.'

'So, which island's it to be?' said the ferryman. 'You've come for the puffins, I suppose.'

'No, no, it's not that,' said Mum. 'We're visiting a friend of mine. She lives on Sloth.'

It was the first time he'd looked remotely serious. 'Really?'

'Yes,' said Mum. 'She's part of a community out there. You must have heard of them. They call themselves the Dawdlers?'

'I've heard of them all right,' said the ferryman. 'I just didn't have you lot down as . . . well, you know.'

'How long will it take?' said Mum. 'To tell you the truth, I'm a bit of a land lubber.'

The ferryman made his way aft and started fiddling with the outboard motor. 'It depends on the sea monsters, of course, but with a bit of luck we should be there in under an hour.' And suddenly he was dead serious again. 'Look, you are sure about this, aren't you? Some of the other islands are quite spectacular.'

'Of course I'm sure,' said Mum. 'Why shouldn't I be? I mean, this thing is completely safe, isn't it?'

'Only three deaths and a missing-presumed-drowned since

January,' he said proudly. 'No, honestly, you'll be fine. I know it looks choppy out there, but this is nothing, believe me.'

'Then why did you ask me if I was sure about it?' said Mum.

'Oh, you know,' said the ferryman. 'It's just . . . Look, we really should get going. Otherwise the tides will change and we'll have to wait here for hours.'

Mum munched hungrily on her bottom lip. 'Then I suppose you'd better —'

The ferryman pulled the ripcord and the motor spluttered into life.

It would have been torture without *Temple Run* on my iPod – as boring as one of those award-winning nature documentaries, except in real time and without the background music or the commentary. Millie would normally have taken it upon herself to lecture us on the school of porpoises that trailed us for a while or the mating habits of the lesser spotted whatdoyoucallit, but she just sat there, like one of those human statues you pay to have your photo taken with outside French cathedrals.

But it was Mum I felt most sorry for. It was bad enough feeling seasick, but it must have been doubly nauseating when the ferryman starting telling her his life story.

' . . . it was one OFSTED inspection too many. That's why I started tutoring. Unfortunately, a certain young gentleman proved particularly . . . challenging, so I came up here to recuperate. This job is only temporary. I'm actually a writer.'

'Oh really,' said Mum, like she'd heard it somewhere before. 'And are you working on something at the moment?'

'I am as it happens. It's a children's book called *Inspectre Horse*.'

Mum was better at lying than Dad, but she still didn't

sound very convincing. 'How interesting.'

'It's about the ghost of a police horse who goes back in time to investigate cases of animal cruelty. These days, publishers prefer a strong concept they can pitch in a single sentence.'

'Yes, well, good luck with it,' said Mum.

I felt like adding 'you'll need it', but as you've seen already, I'm far too polite.

'So, tell me about the Dawdlers,' said Mum. 'You didn't sound very enthusiastic when I mentioned them earlier. What do you know about them?'

'Not a lot,' said the ferryman. 'It all sounds a bit "alternative" for my liking, and apparently their leader chappie's something of a control freak. But to tell you the truth, the anti-technology thing seems eminently reasonable. Although by the look of those two . . .' Millie was still storing up hearing problems for later in life and I'd moved on to *Doodle Jump*. '. . . they might find it a bit of a problem.'

'So, nothing much to worry about, then?' said Mum.

The ferryman pulled hard on the tiller. The little boat lurched to starboard. 'Well, there *was* one thing. Did your friend tell you about the poor lad who died?'

It was news to me, but Mum seemed to know all about it. 'He was the doctor's son, wasn't he? That's why we're here actually. I'm a doctor too, you see. They've asked me to help out for a bit.'

I couldn't resist sticking my oar in. 'What happened to him? How did he . . . ? You know, this kid who . . . ?'

'It was an accident,' said Mum. 'Sue didn't go into details. She was obviously devastated by the whole thing.'

Mum waited for the ferryman to elaborate. He'd bored us

silly with the minute details of his 'idyllic' childhood in Brighton, but now that we'd got on to something interesting, his verbal diarrhoea seemed to have had dried up completely.

'These things happen, I suppose,' said Mum. 'I see it all the time in my line of work.'

The ferryman stared into the gloom. It was at least ten minutes before he finally spoke. 'So, you're a doctor, eh? I don't suppose you'd take a quick look at this rash, would you? Just to make sure it's nothing sinister.'

We spent the rest of the voyage in 'silent contemplation'; the ferryman dreaming up the next thrilling instalment of *Sherlock Horse* and Mum probably racking her brains for a polite way of avoiding his dermatological ailments. I was thinking about Dad. It wasn't that we saw a lot of each other. He worked late so often that we were more like ships that passed in the night. But I always felt safe when I heard his key in the lock and that funny sound he made when he ran upstairs. Now he was miles away and I missed him more than ever.

As for Millie, whatever had upset her, she was a pale copy of the Golden One I had loved and been irritated by for most of my life. It was actually kind of disturbing. Her clear blue eyes had clouded over, and her once open face now wore a 'don't mess with me' scowl. So it was strange that she was the one who broke the silence. 'Look,' she said. 'Over there!'

I'm not sure what came first: the scream of the seagulls or the distant smudge on the horizon. If I'd have known then what I know now, I would have begged the ferryman to take us back, but all I remember is a vague sense of foreboding as The Island of Sloth rose slowly out of the mist.

Part Two

Sloth Welcomes
Careful Dawdlers

Mum's face was slowly returning to its normal colour as we entered the shelter of the bay. 'Thank God for that,' she said. 'I warned you I wasn't much of a sailor.'

The beach looked deserted, apart from a small blue boat with an outboard motor.

'Sorry, chaps, this is it I'm afraid,' said the ferryman. 'I'll take you as close as I can, but unfortunately there's no proper quay or anything.'

'You mean we have to get our feet wet?' I said. 'What about health and safety?' At least I'd picked *something* up from work experience.

The ferryman killed the engine. We drifted slowly towards the shore. 'Weather permitting, I'm back here every fortnight, with a few extra provisions and the mail. If you want a ride to the mainland, that's the best time to catch me.'

'I'll bear it in mind,' said Mum.

'You could still turn back, you know,' he said. 'I'll do you a special offer if you like.'

'Thanks, but no thanks,' said Mum. 'This is probably the best place for us right now.'

The ferryman raised a disgustingly bushy eyebrow. 'You know what they say, don't you? You'll never be happy on an island if it's somewhere you have to run away to.'

'Do they?' said Mum.

'I normally give passengers my mobile number, but that won't be much use to *you*. So if you do have any kind of emergency – not that I'm suggesting for a minute that you will – I think they keep some flares in the fishing boat. You could always try calling me like that.'

'Thanks,' said Mum. 'How much do we owe you?'

'You can pay me on the return journey,' said the ferryman. 'Let's face it, you're not going anywhere.'

The water was freezing. Millie went first, stepping into the shallows without so much as a sharp intake of breath. I screamed louder than a Year Seven girl at a sleepover. Mum wasn't exactly in her comfort zone (that would be a toss-up between a subtitled film about an unhappy art critic, and Marks & Spencer's coffee shop), but with a few words of encouragement from the ferryman, she reluctantly abandoned ship, dragging her suitcase through the white foam with a hysterical smile on her face. 'Thanks a lot,' she called. 'And keep writing.'

We stood and watched the ferry until it was a tiny blob

shrouded in mist. It was only when it disappeared completely that I started to panic.

'I can't believe you've brought us here, Mum. I mean, what do we do now? For all we know, it could be completely deserted. Perhaps Sue made the whole thing up. Dad said she was a bit of a fantasist.'

'Calm down, Jessica,' said Mum. 'You heard what that boring ferry guy said. He'd heard all about them. Look, the whole island's only a few miles long. All we have to do is find their settlement. Isn't that right, Millie?'

Millie was throwing stones at an inquisitive seagull. Mum yanked angrily on her earphones. 'I said, *isn't that right, Millie?*'

'I don't know and I don't care. So just leave me alone, OK? I'm trying to listen.'

Mum put her hand on Millie's shoulder. She wriggled free. 'Look, please, Amelia, I'm begging you. We need to stick together here. Refusing to talk is really not helping.'

'I thought you didn't want me to talk,' said Millie.

'That's not what I meant, and you know it.'

'Well, maybe you'd like me to talk now, then,' said Millie. 'How about I tell —'

It seemed to come from out of nowhere – a familiar voice that brought their 'quiet chat' to a premature conclusion. It was like that on Sloth. What with the mist and the constant moan of the sea, it was very easy for someone to creep up on you.

'You look lost. Can I help you?'

'It's us,' said Mum, rather pathetically.

The voice sounded even more familiar when it went into over-the-top mode. 'OH . . . MY . . . GOD! I didn't recognise you with your hair like that, Mags. This is *so* great! I never thought you'd actually come. But you look like drowned rats, you poor darlings. We'd better get you back to the pods.'

Sue looked older than last time; all seven signs of ageing were now competing for control of her ruddy complexion. And although she still wore the same clothes (jeans, trainers, skiing jacket and a beanie) there was something different about her, something I couldn't quite put my finger on.

'I've been collecting driftwood,' she said, waving a bunch of scabby sticks. 'It's for a special art installation. You know what I said a few years back, about finding my true voice, artistically? Well, I think it's really happening for me.'

Mum was shaking seawater out of her favourite boots. 'I'm so pleased for you.'

'Anyway, enough about me,' said Sue. 'What the hell are you doing here? I know I lose all track of time these days, but the school holidays haven't started yet, have they? And where's David? Working, I suppose?'

Mum squeezed into her soggy boot, like a desperate ugly sister. 'I think, perhaps, before we go anywhere, Sue and I should have a quiet chat.'

'Sounds intriguing,' said Sue, winking at me and Millie before following Mum a little further up the beach.

And while they whispered and hugged, and hugged and whispered, I tried to get a few words out of my sister. 'Are you OK?'

'No, not really.'

'It sucks, I know. But it won't last forever. And Mum seems to think it's for the best. I just wish we knew what Dad thought. You're missing him too, aren't you?'

'*No*,' said Millie, so forcefully I knew she was just putting on a brave face. 'It's not that. I just —'

'OK, you two,' said Sue, bounding over with the fixed grin of a ballroom dancer. 'Let's get this show on the road. Don't worry, girls, it's not too far.'

It was the furthest I'd walked since that sponsored thing round the school field in aid of stand-up comedians, and the narrow muddy path that slalomed up the side of the hill was even more hazardous for Mum's suitcase than the beach.

'Is the weather always like this?' she said.

Sue smiled. 'They say it only rains twice a year: from June to September, and October to May.'

The view from the top of the hill looked a lot better on YouTube.

'Welcome to Sloth,' said Sue, waving her bundle of sticks at the valley below. 'I'm sure you guys are going to love it here.'

'It's beautiful,' said Mum, almost sounding as if she meant it. 'So much greener than it looked on the video.'

'It might take some getting used to,' said Sue. 'Everyone finds the pace of life a bit of a shock to start with.'

'Yes,' said Mum. 'I suppose with all those animals to look after, and what with growing your own vegetables and stuff, it can get a bit frantic.'

'No, Mags, that's not what I —'

'And you live in those funny orangey things, don't you?' I said. 'That is *so* sweet.'

I counted fifteen of them; giant igloos with connecting tubes, like the water slides at the swimming pool, leading to a family of baby igloos.

'We call them the pods,' said Sue. 'They're fully sustainable living spaces, perfectly in tune with the environment.'

'And what about the gigantic blue one in the middle?' said Mum.

'That's the Symposium – our arts and community centre. Where we eat together, meditate together, tell each other stories and make music together.'

'What a load of bollocks,' said Millie.

It was normally my job to embarrass Mum in public. 'Look, I warned you, Amelia. Any more rudeness and you'll be —'

'It's all right,' said Sue. 'A lot of our young people react like that when they first arrive. It soon wears off, believe me.'

'And what are *they*?' I said, pointing at the circle of stones, like a kind of mini Stonehenge but more pointy, on the other side of the valley.

'No one's really sure,' said Sue. 'All we know is they're at least four thousand years old.'

'That's incredible,' said Mum.

'Yeah, incredible,' said Millie. 'If I'd wanted a crap history lesson I'd have asked Mr Catchpole.'

Sue pretended not to hear her. 'They might have been a place of worship, or even human sacrifice. But they're obviously aligned with the sun and the stars, so Earl thinks they're probably some sort of Neolithic weather station.'

'Who's Earl?' said Mum. 'Is he your leader?'

Sue flashed Mum a condescending smile. 'We don't have a leader, Mags. The Dawdlers are a fully autonomous collective. Earl's more like our spokesperson, the voice of our unconscious.'

'I see,' said Mum, who obviously didn't.

'Earl's probably the most talented person you'll ever meet.

Everyone loves him. It was his idea to create a memorial in the middle of the stones.'

'Memorial? What memorial?' I said.

'For Kevin, the young lad who . . .' Sue swallowed hard. '. . . passed away. There's a little wooden cross up there already, but Earl thought it would be fitting if I created something more permanent.' Sue ran a hand through her disgustingly lacklustre hair. 'Anyway, let's get you guys through customs, shall we?'

'Customs?' said Mum. 'This is still part of the British Isles, isn't it? I didn't think we'd need our passports.'

'It's just one of Earl's little jokes,' said Sue. 'No one's allowed up to the pods until one of us has explained our little ways and customs. We don't call them rules; Earl doesn't believe in them.'

'Do we have to do it right now?' said Mum. 'I think we could all do with a couple of hours' sleep. It's been one hell of a journey.'

Sue nodded apologetically. 'It's OK, Mags. I'll take you through myself, if you like. Don't worry, it's quite painless.' Millie was doing an angry, dancey type thing in time to the voice in her head. 'Well, for most people anyway.'

Goodbye to All That

The customs house was a ramshackle wooden hut on the edge of the settlement. We waited outside while Sue went to fetch the master key from Earl.

Mum huddled up against the wall in a vain attempt to shelter from the wind. 'Now please, Millie, when she comes back, for God's sake try not to embarrass me.'

'Is that all you're worried about?' said Millie. 'I would have thought it was the last thing on your mind.'

'Just pull yourself together, all right? Jessica's been very sensible about the whole thing, so why can't you?'

'Yes, but she doesn't —'

'Let's get on with this, shall we?' said Sue, starting to unfasten the first of several padlocks that secured the door. 'I don't know why Earl's so security conscious. There isn't a Dawdler among us who'd be tempted to go back to our old ways.'

There was the tiniest of windows at the far end. I could just make out the contents of the shelves lining the walls: in one corner was a whole stack of Xboxes and PlayStations. (What sort of person took their Xbox to a remote island? Most of the boys at St Thomas's for a start.) Another shelf was entirely devoted to mobiles, with everything from the massive bricks that a few old people still insisted on lugging round as a badge of honour, to the latest smartphone. The colony of iPods and iPads was bad enough, but the real horror movie moment was when I spotted the bucket full of hair straighteners.

'So, how much do you actually know about the Dawdlers?' said Sue, taking her place behind the wooden counter.

'We saw your YouTube video, of course,' said Mum, 'so we know about the technology thing.'

'There's a lot more to it than that, Mags. It's about sustainability and conservation too. For instance, we're planting a whole new forest. We want Sloth to look exactly like it did in the Bronze Age.'

'Super,' said Mum, who probably hadn't used that word since 1984. 'It must be very rewarding.'

Sue took out a shoebox and placed it on the counter. 'It's about preserving this amazingly beautiful world for our children's children.'

'Has anyone got two buckets?' said Millie. 'I think I'm going to be sick. And anyway, *you* haven't got any children.'

'Shut up, Millie,' said Mum.

'But it's not just about the tomorrow,' said Sue, 'it's about today. Childhood is such a precious time. We want our young people to chill out and have fun. Like Earl says, they grow up far too quickly these days. That's why we start by asking you to hand in all your gadgets and gizmos.'

Mum started rummaging in her suitcase. 'OK, well, I'd better go first then. There's my phone, and that's my ereader. I'm halfway through *The Girl with the Dragon Tattoo*. Don't suppose I could hang on to it for a bit?'

'There are plenty of *real* books in the library,' said Sue. 'I'm sure you'll find something more . . . appropriate there.'

Millie tossed her mobile onto the counter without a fight. 'I hope you'll be very happy together.'

I hadn't been anywhere near my phone since the photograph fiasco. And Dad had obviously turned his off to avoid the press. Not being able to talk to him would be agony, but it made handing it over a whole lot easier. When I saw it next to Mum's and Millie's I realised what a crap phone it was anyway.

'Right, how about your mp3 players or any handheld gaming devices?' said Sue.

I'd just started another round of *Temple Run*. 'What am I going to do all day?'

'That's what all the youngsters say to start with,' said Sue. 'A few weeks on Sloth and you'll wonder why you wasted so much precious time on them.'

'You said you wanted us to chill out,' said Millie. 'Well, this is how I do it – listening to music.'

Sue was lining up our phones with the others. 'We make our own music here. And Kirsten holds regular music appreciation sessions in the Symposium.'

'What if I refuse?' said Millie.

'Then, with regret, we'd have to put you straight back on the next ferry.'

'Just give her the bloody thing,' said Mum. 'I'm *not* getting on that boat again in a hurry.'

Millie screwed up her eyes and surrendered herself to the music.

'Come on, love,' said Mum, in that tone she sometimes used with me when threats had proved useless. 'Remember what we're doing this for. It won't be forever, you know.'

Millie screwed up her fist and surrendered her iPod. 'I hate it here already.'

'Thank you, Millie,' said Sue. 'Now how about you, Jess?'

I made one final attempt to escape the demon monkeys before handing it over. 'Looks like I haven't got much choice.'

'I think *you'd* better have this, Mags,' said Sue, handing her the shoebox on the counter. 'It's a bit of a hassle at first, but it really is a great leveller.'

'What's it for?' said Mum.

'Designer labels and slogans; you have to get rid of them. We're all under so much pressure these days to have the latest gear – particularly adolescents. Earl says that no young person should have to suffer because they haven't got the "right" pair of trainers.'

Mum nodded thoughtfully. 'What's in the box exactly?'

'Sewing kit,' said Sue. 'If you can't pick them out, sew a patch over them or stick black tape on the top.'

I suddenly realised what was different about her. She had a scar on the back of her jeans where the label should be, a square of tartan material on the front of her beanie and a strip of black tape across the swoosh on her trainers. The whole effect was kind of spooky.

'I'm afraid this last one can sometimes get a bit emotional,' said Sue solemnly, 'but I promise you, in a couple of weeks, you'll hardly give it another thought.'

'You've got me worried now,' said Mum. 'What is it?'

Sue took off her beanie. Her roots were showing. Whatever colourant she was using, it was a dead loss. She looked like a respectful badger about to break bad news. 'Cosmetics and personal grooming products; it's a multi-million dollar industry based on vanity and greed. We only use what we can find around us.'

I was too shocked to say anything.

Mum sounded almost as traumatised as I was. 'What about hairdryers? You can't possibly mean . . .'

'Of course.' Sue smiled. 'We've got a couple of wind turbines outside the Symposium and a solar-powered lighting system, but there's nowhere to plug them in anyway.'

Mum reached into her suitcase and pulled out her detox and purify hairdryer, laying it out on the counter like the corpse of an old friend.

Millie and I followed suit.

'So that's the lot, is it?' said Sue, doubtfully.

'Oh yes, that's right,' said Mum, handing Sue her styling wand and a salon diffuser. 'I almost forgot I had these.'

My digital hair straighteners joined them on the counter.

Millie's long black hair was perfect; she didn't need them anyway.

'Great, so now it's just beauty products,' said Sue. 'Make-up, shampoo – whatever's your poison.'

'No way,' I said. 'I'm not going anywhere without make-up.

And shampoo's not a beauty product, it's a basic human right.'

'Don't worry,' said Sue. 'There are plenty of natural resources on the island that are actually far less toxic.'

'Could I just keep the ones that haven't been tested on animals, then?' I said. 'I'm sure my mascara's organic.'

Sue smiled and shook her head. 'That's not really the point, Jess. You're a beautiful, intelligent women. You just don't need this stuff. Come on, who's going to be first?'

Mum heaved an industrial-sized jar of anti-ageing cream plus a tube of foundation and an eye-liner pencil onto the counter. 'I've been fighting a losing battle for the last ten years. Maybe it's time to throw in the towel.'

Millie had managed to fit an entire beauty routine into a plastic bag the size of a pencil case. 'There you go,' she said. 'I look like shit anyway.'

It was a technique I'd picked up at school: own up to about fifty per cent of your crimes and misdemeanours, and you can usually get away with the rest. It was probably the hardest choice I'd ever had to make. I could have spent all year on it, and still not came up with the same list twice. 'We didn't have much time to pack,' I said. 'So, this is all I've got, I'm afraid.'

I unzipped my *Where's Wally?* sports bag and started laying out sacrificial cosmetic victims: first the lettuce and juniper face mask, next – and slightly more reluctantly – my second favourite conditioner.

'Is that it?' said Sue.

Just because *she'd* given up fighting, didn't mean that Mum had to drop *me* in it. 'Come on, Jess,' she said. 'You're telling me you haven't got some shampoo in their somewhere?'

'You saw what happened when Ella tried that "no-poo"

thing,' I said. 'It was absolutely disgusting.'

'We make our own out of baking soda and seaweed,' said Sue. 'It's more of a paste really, but it's just as effective as anything you can buy in the shops.'

'*OK*,' I said, putting on the poker face that Dad taught me on that waterlogged weekend in a so-called luxury caravan when he forced us to learn gin rummy. 'This really *is* everything.' I played my crackle nail varnish first, next, a beautifully acted yelp of pain followed by my Soft and Silky Salon Results shampoo. And finally, in what felt like my cleverest move yet (especially if it meant hanging on to my foundation and mascara), the packet of sanitary towels. I didn't dare think what the Dawdler alternative might be.

Sue reached across the counter and grabbed my sports bag. 'Sorry, Jess, but I think I'd better make sure that you haven't missed anything.'

'Give me that. You can't just —'

'Look, if we're going to do this, I think we'd better do it properly,' said Mum.

'Oh yeah, that's right. Treat her like a kid, why don't you?' said Millie. 'What gives you the right, anyway?'

For one glorious minute it looked like she'd missed my anti-frizz serum. A few seconds later it was lying on a pile with my Big It Up conditioner, my grape and pomegranate cleanser and all the rest of my beauty products.

'OK, OK, fine,' I said. 'But *please* just let me keep my mascara.'

'Sorry, but it's the same for everyone, I promise,' said Sue. 'And I'm afraid I'm going to have to ask for the bag too. Don't worry, I'll find you another one.'

'No way,' I said, grabbing back my *Where's Wally?* sports bag and holding it close to my chest. 'What do you want it for, anyway?'

'It's a brand, isn't it?' said Sue. 'Well, a franchise anyway.'

'You're not having it,' I said. 'You can take everything else, but you're not having my bag.'

It wasn't especially cool for someone in Year Ten to be carrying a *Where's Wally?* sports bag. There were a couple of Year Sevens who thought it was hilarious to enquire after Wally's whereabouts whenever they saw me. But I didn't care. I'd had that bag since primary school and I wasn't giving it up for anybody.

'What's so special about it?' said Sue. 'I mean, it's not exactly Gucci, is it?'

'Dad gave it to me,' I said. 'You can say what you like, but you're not having it.'

'Please, Sue,' said Mum, suddenly on my side for once. 'It's only a bag.'

OK,' said Sue. 'Just make sure you wear Wally on the inside so no one can see him. Oh and you'd better have these too.' She handed me back the sanitary towels. 'Earl says we should use something recyclable, but most of the women think that's taking things a bit far!'

'Right, thanks,' I said, wishing they'd felt more strongly about eye-liner.

'Anyway, let's get you to your pod, shall we?' said Sue. 'I bet you can't wait to meet some of our amazing young people.'

I had a feeling they'd be a bit like that weird girl in Year Eleven who wore hand-knitted jumpers and refused to wear make-up.

If only.

Aquiescent Adolescents

'The last crofters left Sloth in 1957,' said Sue, 'but if you look up on the moor you can just make out the remains of an old blackhouse. They called their dwellings blackhouses because the open peat fires stained the walls.' She pointed to a row of brightly coloured beach huts. 'And those are the composting toilets. Rather fun, aren't they? You'll find some buckets of sawdust in the shed round the back.'

Luckily my mind was otherwise engaged. I was trying to imagine a world without mascara; trying to convince myself it wasn't the dystopian nightmare that every other film I'd seen that year, not to mention Mrs Woolf's English lessons, had led me to expect. I was half succeeding until we arrived at the pods, and a bleak vision of the future walked – very slowly – across our path.

'Oh look,' said Sue. 'It's Derek and the Striplings.'

'They sound like a sixties pop group,' said Mum, bravely attempting to disguise her horror.

'Earl's not keen on the expression "teenager",' said Sue. 'He says it's nothing more than a cynical marketing ploy. That's why we call our young adults the Striplings. As you can see, Derek's taking them through a walking meditation.'

There is nothing at all unusual about middle-aged fashion disasters. They all look the same to me. So the man in the disgustingly baggy shorts, blue anorak and clown-sized walking boots was no more unsettling than Mr Catchpole's infamous denim jacket.

'That's great, folks,' he said, beaming proudly as the 'amazing young people' turned every step into a five-act tragedy with eighty pages of footnotes. (Footnotes – get it?) 'Now I want you to feel grounded. Just stay in the moment; that's what it's all about.'

No, the disturbing part of the vision wasn't Derek, it was his so-called Striplings, who were parading in front of us like a creep of unfashionable tortoises.

'Amazing, isn't it?' said Sue. 'Some of this lot were so chronically addicted to twenty-first century toxicity when they first arrived they could barely function unless they were doing three things at once.'

It was wrong on so many levels. Most of them looked about my age, with maybe a couple of older ones thrown in. How was it then that all eight Striplings were taking the slow-motion walking thing so seriously? What self-respecting St Thomas's kid would have passed-up the opportunity to exchange libellous banter and wedges of bubble gum behind the teacher's back?

But if the boys looked like a mad Victorian barber had assaulted them with a blunt pair of manually operated hedge clippers, the girls were simply unspeakable. Pastier than movie vampires, but without the quirky fashion sense or perfect skin tone, their greasy hair hung lankly about their faces, giving them the appearance of undernourished rescue ponies.

'Good afternoon,' said the knobbly kneed meditation teacher, bounding towards Mum with his hand outstretched. 'I'm Derek. Welcome to Sloth.'

Mum winced as he pumped her hand. 'Thanks very much.'

'This is my dear friend, Maggie,' said Sue. 'She's the doctor I talked about in the Symposium.'

'That's splendid,' said Derek, 'but Sue seemed to think you weren't coming. How long do you think you'll be here? And what made you change your mind?'

Mum stared at her favourite boots. 'Well, I don't know, I —'

'*Anyway*, I haven't introduced the girls yet,' said Sue. 'This is Millie and that's Jessica.'

'Two more Striplings, I see,' said Derek. 'I expect you want to unpack right now, but don't worry, you'll both be joining us tomorrow morning. I'll try and plan something special for your first day.' He must have detected my super-sized misgivings. They were like the Great Wall of China; an astronaut could have spotted them from outer space. 'Don't worry, Jessica; it's nothing like school. We're not an exam factory. And you won't find any bullying here. Our youngsters are the nicest bunch you're ever likely to come across.'

I wanted to believe him. Unfortunately, from where I was

standing, the prognosis wasn't good. When a new kid arrived at St Thomas's, at least we gave them the benefit of the doubt until we'd seen their Facebook page. This lot treated all my attempts to make contact with zombie-like indifference. I smiled, practically pouted like a porn star, and got nothing, not even the slightest nod of recognition, in return. I didn't want to jump to conclusions, but they could quite easily have been the kind of teenagers who fought to the death in state-sponsored killing competitions, or at the very least wrote short stories and played a musical instrument freakishly well.

'We'd better get going,' said Sue. 'Once I've settled these guys into their pod, Earl thinks they could probably do with an afternoon nap.'

Just as we were turning to leave, I made a bit of a breakthrough.

He would have been OK-looking with decent clothes, better skin and a hairstyle from the twenty-first century. In fact, the boy in the disgustingly grubby jumper with the cute nose and soft beginnings of what might many years from now blossom into a credible moustache, had a lot going for him. That's why I wasn't exactly heartbroken when I realised he was checking me out.

At least that's what I thought. *Teach Yourself Flirting* decreed that after returning his gaze for a nanosecond, I should look away and do that simpering thing I've always been so crap at. But when I turned back, expecting a full on smile, he was staring at his feet like all the rest.

'There's just one little thing before you go,' said Derek, sidling up to Mum and lowering his voice to a conspiratorial whisper. 'I don't know if it's the organic diet or what, but the thing is I'm having a bit of trouble with my . . .'

Mum got quite cross when the people she met in town wanted medical advice. ('I mean, you wouldn't ask an off-duty plumber to unblock your toilet.') I couldn't hear what Derek said next, but judging from Mum's face it was the sort of embarrassing ailment you saw most weeks on a documentary.

Derek, on the other hand, looked much chirpier after his free consultation. 'Well, that's a relief, I must say. Anyway, I'll let you good people get on. And we'll see you two girls tomorrow morning outside the Symposium.'

'Over my dead body,' muttered Millie.

Hopefully it wouldn't come to that. But from what I'd seen already, the alternative didn't look much better.

We Need
To Talk About Kevin

The pods were the opposite of the Tardis: smaller than they looked when you got inside.

'This is your living area,' said Sue. 'Don't get me wrong, Mags, the communal aspects of Dawdler life are incredibly rewarding. It's just nice to have a room of your own to hang out in once in a while.'

'There's so much more space without a television, isn't there?' said Mum, casting her eye over the grim collection of second-hand furniture, the depressing family of purple beanbags and the black hole where the telly should have been.

'Now, how about I show you to your sleeping area, Mags?'

'*No*,' said Mum, her happy camper act starting to falter. 'I think I'd better stay here and get to work on these labels. Why don't you show the girls to their room first?'

Sue led us down the narrow connecting tube until we came to a baby pod just tall enough to stand up in.

'Cosy, isn't it?' said Sue, flicking on the solar-powered lighting system, which failed to throw much more light on the situation than the tiny porthole in the roof. It was probably just as well. The cheap chest of drawers, two lumpy futons and a cold grey colour scheme made Death Row look like The Ritz.

'Wake me up when it's all over,' said Millie, selecting a futon and pulling the scratchy woollen blanket over her head.

It was the first time we'd shared a room since Portugal. She'd made a right old fuss about my 'disgusting habit' of burying the floor with my underwear, and insisted on drawing up a cleaning rota for the ensuite shower. This time last year she would have been allocating cupboard space.

'I'd better take the other one, then,' I said, dumping my *Where's Wally?* sports bag on the futon and sitting down next to it. 'Hang on a minute, what's this?'

'What's what?' said Sue.

'This poster.' Blu-tacked to the wall, just above my head, was a photograph of an old-fashioned fishing boat with a painting of a white bird across its bows. 'What's the Rainbow Warrior anyway?'

'Don't you know anything?' came Millie's muffled voice from under the blanket. 'Rainbow Warrior was a campaigning vessel for the environmental organisation Greenpeace. Haven't you ever heard of Save the Whale?'

'Oh no,' whispered Sue, tugging at her disgustingly visible roots. 'I'm so sorry. That really shouldn't be here.'

'Don't worry about it,' I said. 'It's only a poster. I quite like it actually.'

Sue dabbed her face with a recycled tissue. 'You don't understand. It belonged to Kevin. We were supposed to pack up all his things after he . . . after he . . .'

'Oh . . . right,' I said, suddenly realising why she'd gone all weird. 'Kevin was the boy who died, was he?'

Sue sniffed and nodded. 'That poster was so typical of him. He wasn't interested in millionaire footballers or shallow celebrities. He'd really embraced the whole Dawdler philosophy.'

'What exactly happened to him, Sue?'

'It was an accident, a freak accident up on the north cliffs. Look, I really should take that poster.'

'It's fine,' I said. 'Kind of brightens the place up.'

'Earl says we shouldn't live in the past,' said Sue, peeling the Rainbow Warrior off the wall and rolling it into a tight tube. 'After every tragedy, the moment comes when it's time to move on. It's more difficult for him, of course.'

'What do you mean?'

'Earl was the one who found him,' said Sue. 'It's been over two months now, but I know he still has nightmares about it, poor guy.'

And I was half wondering if Earl shared the contents of his nightmares with the whole community, when a horrible scream rang out from the mother pod. 'Mum!' I shouted. 'Mum, are you OK?'

We raced back down the tunnel. Even Millie pulled the blanket around her and stumbled after us, like the loser in the sack race.

Mum was standing on her suitcase with a blacked-out trainer in her hand. 'It was huge,' she whimpered. 'I've never seen anything like it.'

'Has one of those saddos been giving you grief?' said Millie.

'It was behind the beanbag,' said Mum. 'Then it scuttled across the room – bold as brass.'

Sue reverted back to the irritatingly optimistic tour guide. 'It's just one of the rats, you silly old thing.'

'Rats!' I squealed. 'That's disgusting. You're not telling me this place is infested, are you?'

'Don't worry, Jess, these are brown rats,' said Sue. 'They'll be eating out of your hand in no time.'

It sounded like my worst nightmare. Throw in a couple of snakes and a disastrous poodle-perm and you'd have been spot on.

'Oh dear God,' said Mum. 'Why did I bring you here?'

'You know why,' said Millie, darkly.

'Look, I know this must be really hard for you, Mags, but it will get better I promise.' Sue backed slowly towards the entry hatch. 'Anyway, why don't you guys catch up on some sleep this afternoon and I'll see you in the Symposium for dinner tonight.'

'What time?' said Mum.

'We don't have set times here. Earl plays a couple of riffs on his saxophone when it's ready.'

Mum tried to dredge up a smile. 'Sounds like the neighbour from hell.'

'Which reminds me,' said Sue. 'I forgot to take your watches. We do our best to live in harmony with nature. Earl can't stand clock-watchers.'

I barely murmured as I handed her the silver watch Grandma gave me for my thirteenth birthday. What was the point in knowing the time if no one else did?

'I'll leave you to it, then,' said Sue, tucking Mum's travel clock into her jeans pocket. 'The food here's amazing by the way; all locally sourced and completely organic. Not only that, you'll get to meet Earl, of course. That man is *so* charismatic it's untrue. You're going to love him, guys, I know you are.'

Personally, I had my doubts.

My Name Is Earl

I'll never forget the smell in the Symposium. You got used to it after a while, but that first night there were times when I was an organic parsnip away from throwing up. It reminded me of that vegetarian restaurant in Brighton, except with a pungent mixture of mud, sweat and animal droppings thrown in. Considering they were only allowed four – quite often lukewarm – showers a week, it was hardly surprising some of the Dawdlers were a bit whiffy. They worked long hours in the fields or out in the fishing boat, and the ban on commercial deodorants meant the evidence lingered about the Symposium like a . . . well, like a bad smell.

We sat at long trestle tables arranged around a circular wooden platform, while an amateur army of waiters and waitresses (everyone in the community took their turn) brought us steaming bowls of gloop that the 'cooking team' had ladled from a giant cauldron.

'This is pathetic,' said Millie. 'Why can't we just start?'

'I told you,' said Sue. 'Earl likes to say a few words first. It's a Dawdler tradition.'

Mum was wearing the navy-blue trouser suit that was such a bargain in the Easter sales. It always made me sad, the way she insisted on dressing up every time we went out to eat, like she was trying too hard or something. And it was even sadder without Dad to make veiled comments about the price tag.

'Yes, come on, Millie,' said Mum. 'When in Rome and all that.'

'We're not *in* Rome,' said Millie. 'It looks disgusting anyway.'

There were about fifty Dawdlers in all, including a bunch of primary school kids who were known as the 'Junior Laggards' and a couple of babies. Most of the adults were disgustingly friendly, but I couldn't help noticing that not one of the eight Striplings popped over to introduce themselves.

Sue's face shone brighter than the solar-powered lighting system when the man in a crumpled linen suit and logo-less skate shoes leaped on to the stage. 'It's Earl,' she whispered. 'Isn't he amazing?'

Her geriatric crush was almost as sickening as the vegetables, but it has to be said that, for a man of his age, Earl was in pretty good shape. In fact, he looked better in the flesh than he did on YouTube. His shoulder length mane was flecked with silver and in far better condition than it had any right to be, and his voice was cool and gravelly, like of one of those 'dad rock' guys that Mum got so nostalgic about.

'Allrightee,' he said, turning slowly through three hundred and sixty degrees, giving everyone the benefit of his perfect teeth. 'As I hope you all know by now, my name is Earl.'

From the way they all laughed you'd have thought he was the funniest thing since the 'holiday armadillo' episode of *Friends*.

'Before we eat, I want to give a special Dawdler welcome to Maggie, our new doctor, and her two lovely daughters, Jessica and Millie. I'm sure they're going to be great assets to our little community. Stand up will you, guys?'

Millie buried her head in her hands whilst me and Mum stood reluctantly to receive the customary slow handclap.

'OK, thanks, guys, you can sit down now.' Earl paused for a moment, his flawless smile turning into something altogether more serious. 'I know they only came here because of . . . what happened to Kevin, so I wanted to share something with all of you. A few days ago, I had a letter from Douglas and Janet.'

A tense hush fell over the Symposium.

'It's early days of course, but they both felt it would be a tremendous pity if a tragic accident was to overshadow some of the wonderful things we've achieved here.' He stared into the distance. It was probably a trick of the solar-powered lighting system, but I could have sworn his left temple was twitching. 'That's all really. So come on guys, let's eat.'

Millie was right, the food *was* disgusting: the organic vegetables were so deformed they were practically unrecognisable, and the monkfish was chewier than the bulletproof bread. We normally ate in front of the telly – except when Grandma came or the odd Sunday lunch. It didn't feel right without talking heads in the background, and it was even worse when Helga and Toby, the couple on the bench opposite, tried starting a conversation about the environmental implications of air travel. So I felt quite relieved when the last remains of baked apple with goat's cheese had been cleared away and Earl jumped onto the stage again.

'Now, tomorrow's weather. Looks like we'll be starting with a heavy mist, but don't worry. It should clear by mid-morning. Which is great news for Derek, because a little bird tells me he's got something special planned for the Striplings.'

'Told you he was amazing, didn't I?' whispered Sue. 'He's so *in tune* with the island he can even predict the weather.'

'Yeah, because it's never misty on a Scottish island, is it?' said Millie. 'Give the guru a coconut!'

'OK, people,' said Earl. 'Before we meditate, there's someone here who wants to bend your ears for a minute. Now, for the benefit of the new guys, once a month we ask a member of the community to step up here and share a few thoughts about the "Dawdler experience". And it's particularly exciting when one of our young people feels really passionate about the work we're doing. So, I'm sure you'll all want to join me in welcoming Campbell to the stage.'

It was *him* – the boy outside the pods who'd been checking me out. He still wore the same skanky jumper, and his skin looked even more disastrous close-up. On the other hand, he was taller than I remembered and there was something borderline cute about his shy smile, which he managed to keep going right through the longest slow handclap in history. Unfortunately, the moment he opened his mouth, I started going off him.

'When we first, *like*, came here, I was, *like*, your totally typical teenager?'

He paused, winking nauseatingly to reassure the audience

that his witty repetition of the word 'like' and the upward inflection at the end of the sentence (the 'Aussie soap thing' that Dad kept complaining about) was deliberate.

'You know what I mean,' he said. 'Two thousand friends on Facebook and not one person you can really talk to. That's the trouble with technology. There's nowhere to hide. You carry it around in your pocket all day, and then when you get home from school you're too frightened to log out in case something exciting starts trending on Twitter.'

Some of the Dawdlers nodded approvingly.

'I didn't know it at the time, but I was actually really unhappy. There's this unbelievable pressure to keep getting the latest, fastest must-have item: latest phone, latest video game, latest fibre-optic broadband. But when you get hold of it, you feel good for about two seconds, and then it's time to trade it in for an upgrade.'

'Yeah, you're so right,' came a voice from the back of the Symposium.

'I bought into the celebrity culture thing too. It's like you can't be happy unless you're famous or you look like a fashion model. You should have seen all the gunk I put in my hair. I was sixteen years old, but I was so worried about my appearance that I actually started using anti-ageing moisturiser!'

For some reason this got a few laughs. I couldn't help thinking he should have stuck with it.

'School was just as bad. It was never a case of learning for the sheer joy of it, like we do here. It was all about private tutors and A stars in the next exam. No wonder I was addicted to fast food. Pizza, burgers . . . subs. You name it, I was into it.'

I was so hungry after that revolting monkfish, I was practically drooling.

'These days my diet is completely additive-free, and I've got to tell you, I'm really loving it. So I want to thank Earl and all you guys for letting me be part of this exciting experiment. If it wasn't for you, I'd probably be up in my bedroom right now, playing violent video games, tweeting rubbish to a troop of imaginary followers, listening to so-called "music" . . .' [He did that quote marks gesture that no one had done in real life for at least a decade.] '. . . and pigging out on pepperoni pizza.'

A slow handclap was starting to build.

'Learning to meditate has probably been the most rewarding part of the whole journey. It's been over six months now, and I've just about learned to slow down and start living in the moment. And you know what? It's as if I finally got my childhood back.'

At this, the Dawdlers pounded on the tables, like the end of a feel-good movie where the eccentric band of losers stop the multi-national corporation turning their butterfly sanctuary into a shopping mall.

'Sanctimonious little freak,' said Millie.

It was true; there was something just a little bit too self-satisfied about the triumphant smile which he appeared to direct at some of his fellow Striplings. If they were anything like Campbell, I wouldn't even accept their friendship requests on Facebook.

'Thank you for listening,' he said, bringing his hands together and bowing his head. 'Oh, before I go, Earl asked me to mention that he knows how keen you are to start meditating, but to avoid silly accidents, could we please give Erika and the Junior Laggards a couple of minutes to make their way to the puppet show in the library? Thanks a lot.'

The young kids skipped across to the entry hatch, waving happily at their parents. The moment they'd gone, everyone started dragging tables to the sides of the Symposium and Earl and Derek lugged an enormous candle, like the kind you saw in churches, onto the stage.

'Grab hold of that would you, Jess?' said Sue, offering me one end of the bench. 'It doesn't take long if we all pitch in.'

'What's that candle for?' I said.

'It helps to have something to focus on,' said Sue. 'When it burns down to the black line, it means the meditation session's over.'

'Well, I'm not bloody doing it,' said Millie. 'What's the point anyway?'

Sue smiled condescendingly. 'You heard what Campbell said. It's about being in the moment. We spend most of our lives either living in the past or worrying about the future. If you can train your mind to stay in one place for a change, it's actually very liberating.'

'Oh . . . right,' said Millie, thoughtfully.

The Dawdlers began claiming their places on the drafty wooden floor. Sue led us to her favourite spot in front of the over-sized cauldron. 'It's warmer here,' she whispered.

'Don't we need some kind of instruction first?' said Mum.

Sue smiled even more condescendingly. 'Meditation is the easiest thing in the world, and the hardest too. Just focus on your breathing, Mags, and see where it takes you.'

It was typical of the Striplings that they kept themselves to themselves. They sat in a tight group, just in front of the entrance hatch.

'OK, is everybody ready for this?' said Earl, advancing

towards the candle with a lighted taper in his hand. 'Now remember, guys, this isn't a competition. And, for the benefit of the newbies, *nothing* we do here is compulsory. If it all gets a bit intense, why not step outside for a couple of minutes? But try and stick with it if you can. Because, believe me, there's no greater gift than a quiet mind.'

The candle flamed impressively and someone killed the lights. Once Earl had taken his place in the inner circle, the hushed quiet became an excruciating silence. I could sense Mum's embarrassment as the people around her began withdrawing into a kind of narrow-eyed trance. Sue was predictably 'transcendental', but the real surprise was Millie. With her tiny wrists balanced on her knees, and her index fingers and thumbs clasped so tightly it looked like she was squashing insects, I had the feeling she was totally into it.

But I wasn't. The first few minutes lasted a lifetime. There was nothing very liberating about sitting cross-legged in a giant bubble with a bunch of cosmetically-challenged statues and only the wind to puncture the silence. All I could do was worry about the future, and meditate on the past: Why was Millie acting so strangely? What horrendous activity had Derek planned for the Striplings tomorrow? Did the girl with split ends fancy Campbell? Were said split ends the direct result of baking soda and seaweed hair paste? And if all Mum wanted was to escape from a couple of journalists, what possessed her to drive over five hundred miles to the land that time forgot?

But wherever my mind wandered, it kept coming back to Dad. How was he coping without us? When would we see him again? How did he feel about the three of us taking off like that? It was so upsetting that I made a conscious decision to try and stop thinking about him. But I was already wondering if Grandma was winding him up about politics yet, when an unexpected development whisked me back to the here and now. Because what I saw didn't make sense. If meditation was so rewarding, how come the Striplings seemed to be making a mass exit? It might not have been compulsory, but if Campbell was such a born again Dawdler, what was he doing holding open the entrance hatch and waving them through?

They seemed to be gone for hours. In reality it was more like twenty-five minutes before they returned, slipping back into the Symposium just moments before the candle burned down to the black mark.

'OK, guys, see you tomorrow,' said Earl. 'I hope that was enlightening.'

It was the second time in as many hours that I'd parked my bum on a scratchy wooden surface while the wind whistled about my nether regions. I was keen to keep my first visit to the composting toilets as short as possible, but the more desperate I became to get out of there (and let me tell you, Sue had a pretty strange idea of what 'completely odourless' meant), the harder it was to get started.

However, I *was* shitting myself about the next morning. Sloth might not have had a lot in common with St Thomas's, but whichever way you looked at it, it was still my first day at a new school – and I knew what that meant. If the other kids didn't like you, it was the beginning of a whole new chapter of misery that could last until prom night. I still remembered what they'd done to the girl with 'funny ears' in Year Eight. And the Striplings weren't exactly your average teenagers. Never mind putting chewing gum in your hair and fraping your profile; who knew what screwy stuff they were dreaming up for Millie and me?

Mission finally accomplished, I threw a bucket of sawdust down the toilet and made a break for the pods.

The island was full of noises. Like I said, the roar of the sea was the background to everything, but on top of that there was the weeping wind, the crying gulls, the high-pitched screams of the arctic terns and a whole chorus of farm animals. You learned to live with it in the end, but my first walk back from the composting toilets left me jumpier than a kangaroo on the verge of a nervous breakdown.

There was human music too. I soon learned that, like Grandma, the Dawdlers had this weird obsession about making their own entertainment. A string quartet gave regular recitals, the choir had a nasty habit of launching into after-dinner ballads about dying Viking princesses, a guitarist called Rick often sat outside the composting toilets playing the blues – and then of course there was Earl's saxophone. Every evening it summoned us to the Symposium, and in the morning it dragged you from your slumbers with a reedy, wake-up medley. I never knew any of the songs he played, although according to Mum, the sax solo from 'Baker Street' was a seventies classic.

But that night, I heard the saddest song of all. Wordless though it was, the rich soulful voices of the performers spoke to me so powerfully it was almost like they understood my loneliness, shared in my pain. Or was it a warning? I only wished I could ask them face to face. A few days later, I had my chance. They were basking on the rocks beneath the north cliffs. I'd always planned on 'Another One Bites the Dust', but it would be kind of cool to have a colony of seals sing at my funeral.

'Was it OK, love?' said Mum.

I yanked the entry hatch shut, trying for Mum's benefit to sound a whole lot more positive than I actually felt. 'Yeah, kind of; as long as you watch what you're treading in.'

'How about the recycled paper?'

'Bit scratchy, but I suppose you get used to it.'

The purple beanbag was haemorrhaging badly. Mum looked pretty uncomfortable with her legs pulled tight against her chest. 'You will be all right, won't you, Jess?'

'I think so.'

'I'm really proud of you, you know. You've been . . . amazing.'

Amazing wasn't a word she often used about me ('amazingly rude', perhaps). I sat on the arm of the chair, resting my hand gently on her shoulder. 'What about you, Mum? Will *you* be all right?'

'We'll see after tomorrow. I get the feeling the health centre isn't exactly state-of-the-art.'

'No, I meant about . . . well, you know.'

She reached up and squeezed my hand. 'I don't know, love. I really don't know.'

'Maybe you should get some sleep, Mum. You look exhausted.'

She pulled her knees tighter to her chest. 'What with all those rats about?'

It was my turn to fob *her* off with a classic adult lie. 'Don't worry, I expect they're more scared of us than we are of them.'

'Oh, you think so?'

She still smelled of her old perfume. In a few days she'd be 'completely odourless'. 'Mum?' I said, squeezing into the chair beside her. 'Do you mind if I ask you something?'

'Course not.'

'When can we go home? How long will it take Dad to sort things out?'

'I don't know,' said Mum, vacating her beanbag and faking a yawn. 'But you know what? Maybe you're right. Maybe I *should* try and get a few hours' sleep. And you ought to do the same, Jess.' She leaned over and kissed the top of my head. 'Try not to wind up your sister, eh? She's not really herself at the moment.'

You could say that again. Millie had turned into such a snarling ball of fury that as I crawled down the tunnel towards our bedroom, I was kind of hoping she'd be asleep. The last thing I expected was to find her sitting up in bed with a contented smile on her face.

'Look what I've got,' she said, waving it at me, like a baby-faced assassin.

'What is it?'

'What does it look like?'

'And where did you find it?'

'Sue gave it to me.'

It felt so good to be having a regular conversation with her that I wasn't going to ruin it all by casting any further doubts on Sue's sanity. 'Oh yeah, what for?'

'So I can help with her art installation. She's going to teach me carving. I've always been interested in that kind of thing. I've just never had the time before.'

I was genuinely pleased that Millie had a new project, but it still felt wrong to see the Golden One with a knife in her hand.

Nature Dawdle

Derek's stretching routine reminded me of the pilates DVD that Mum did religiously until about the fourth of January. Balancing shakily on one leg, he clung to the side of the Symposium, using the other hand to yank his ankle towards his bum.

'What time do lessons start?' I said, realising I should have waited longer after Earl's wake-up riff if I'd wanted to be fashionably late.

'As soon as everyone's here,' said Derek. 'I mean, we don't call a register or anything! And we don't really call them lessons either. You'll probably find it hard to start with, Jessica, but try not to think of me as a teacher; try to think of me more as a friend.'

I remembered Mr Catchpole saying almost exactly the opposite to Aidan Corcoran.

'I know you're probably dying to get to know them,' said Derek, dropping into a lunge. 'Don't worry, they're a keen old bunch. I'm sure they'll be here soon.'

'Good,' I lied.

Derek forced his fingertips to within spitting distance of his walking boots. 'Where's your sister, by the way?'

'She's not coming. I think she's got . . . an upset stomach or something. Should Mum have written her a note?' Well, it was kinder than relaying Millie's message about Derek being a fat-arsed loser who couldn't teach a ten-year-old to pick his nose.

'Don't worry about it,' said Derek. 'Nothing here's compulsory anyway – although Earl does prefer everyone to participate as fully as possible.'

'Thanks,' I said. 'I'll tell her.'

'Anyway, it looks like we're in luck. Here's our first customer.'

One by one they stepped out of the mist, and Derek introduced us. There was nothing unusual about their names: Molly, Jack, Edward and Naseeb – plus the obligatory brace of Harrys (M and W). What did feel pretty un-St Thomas's-like was the way each one of them shook my hand, greeted me with a formal 'Good morning, Jessica' and slunk back into the mist.

Campbell and Lucy showed up last. I'd already taken a dislike to Lucy. There was something disgustingly holier than thou about the way she'd changed the label on her hoodie to *HOLISTIC*, and her natural curls looked unnaturally well-nourished considering the absence of any kind of hair and beauty routine.

I'd have loved to have taken Campbell shopping. Even a

supermarket own brand exfoliator would have improved his complexion, and a black dustbin-liner couldn't have been any worse than that terrible jumper. Our introduction was a disappointment too. I was kind of hoping he'd give me a little squeeze or at the very least a shy smile, but his handshake was as lifeless as a dead salmon.

'Now, I thought it would be a nice idea if we spent this morning introducing Jessica to her new home,' said Derek. 'So what I suggest is that we take a leisurely nature ramble – or rather "nature dawdle" . . .' He grinned impishly; the Striplings chuckled. '. . . around the island. How does that sound to everybody?'

If I needed any further confirmation that they were not your average teenagers, it came in their ecstatic reaction to Derek's lesson plan.

'We can show Jessica the aspens and willows we planted,' said Jack.

'We want Sloth to look just like it did in the Bronze Age,' added Naseeb.

'If we're lucky, the vetch daisies will be out,' said Molly.

Lucy was excited about the prospect that the fulmars might be nesting – whatever they were.

And I was probably imagining it, but I'm sure I heard someone say 'smashing'.

'It won't be the kind of school outing you're used to.' Derek smiled. 'For a start, I shan't be complaining if anyone lags behind. In fact, I always encourage the Striplings to do their own thing.'

I remembered Mr Catchpole saying almost exactly the opposite to Aidan Corcoran.

'Let's get going, then,' said Derek, obviously forgetting to remind us that while we were out dawdling we were of course ambassadors of the school.

Now I've been on about half a million school trips – from the war graves of Flanders to the cheese factories of middle-England, and more heritage sites and creative writing workshops than I'd care to remember. And the one thing I *have* learned is that they'd all be totally rubbish without your friends. Who could possibly forget Ella's Beyoncé impression on the coach back from the Science Museum or the time we convinced Miss Hoolyhan that Aidan Corcoran had gone backstage at the National Theatre?

Derek's dawdle proved my point. The other kids quickly paired off (Campbell with Lucy again, I couldn't help noticing) and I was left to bring up the rear with a man at least forty years too old to be wearing short trousers, and with a warped idea of what would fascinate me. 'Do you realise those stones date right back to four thousand BC, Jessica – isn't that incredible?' I was actually more interested in the simple wooden cross that lay in their midst.

And the Striplings were just as bad, turning back every few minutes to express their enthusiasm for a rare heather or identify yet another feature of the 'magnificent wildlife'.

'Great news,' shouted Derek, pointing at a distant dot on the horizon. 'I do believe the puffins are back. Come on, we'll get a better view from the top of the cliffs.'

Earl was certainly right about the weather. Now the mist had cleared you could see forever. If you were unlucky enough to be cornered by one of Sue's watercolourists, they'd sometimes go off on one about the 'extraordinary quality of light'.

Right from the start, I could kind of appreciate that the

island was beautiful, but what struck me more was its natural cruelty. From the tumultuous North Atlantic breakers frothing up white against the stark, grey coastline, to the vicious wind that would have felt no conscience about sending the whole pack of us hurtling to a watery grave, it seemed designed to be as unwelcoming as possible. And it was the same with the wildlife. Underneath all that grace and fluffiness, it was basically a case of kill or be killed. Those performing seals might have looked cute, but they were vicious predators who guarded their territory with sadistic intensity. Tramping through the mushy marram grass towards the point at which the land met the sky, I couldn't help wondering if the Striplings were the same.

'Good,' gasped Derek, slipping off his rucksack and taking refuge behind one of the enormous boulders that lay strewn along the clifftop. 'I'll get lunch ready, while you guys have a quick look round.'

It was a health and safety nightmare. Dad's faithful assistant, Brian Simkins, would have written a thousand page risk assessment. Campbell and the others marched fearlessly forwards, standing to attention about five metres from the edge. A flock of oversized seagulls hovered menacingly, their hoarse cries conjuring painful memories of Miss Hoolyhan's chamber choir.

'Watch out for those fulmars,' shouted Derek. 'If they think you're trying to steal their eggs, they'll swoop down and vomit out a red rust dye.'

Campbell turned back and waved. I was sure I heard giggling.

'Well, go on, Jessica,' said Derek. 'Don't you want to join them?'

My heart screamed no no, no no, no no, no no; my head whispered exactly the opposite. There was a sheer drop of what must have been at least a hundred metres onto the jagged rocks below. I was so scared of heights I could barely manage to stand on the bench at the back of the school photograph. But I knew that to betray any sign of weakness would leave me as vulnerable as a baby penguin in a colony of ravenous seals.

'Yes. Right. Good idea,' I said, edging slowly towards them, my hair streaming – but not remotely attractively – in the wind.

The giggling stopped as I inched into the gap between Lucy and Campbell.

'Hello, Jessica,' said Lucy, sounding about as welcoming as a venomous lizard. 'How are you enjoying yourself?'

'Not a lot,' I said. 'In fact, if you really want to know, I'm a bit bored.'

Another giggle, and the suspicion of whispering down the line.

'What's the matter?' said Campbell. 'Missing our iPod, are we? Can't live without a mobile telephone?'

The others chipped in with some 'amusing' suggestions of their own.

'Getting withdrawal symptoms because you missed the latest episode of *Celebrity Brain Transplant*?' said Molly.

'Dying for a burger?' said Jack.

'Dying for a tweet, more like,' said Naseeb.

'*No*,' I said, trying desperately not to look down. 'I'm just not that into nature, OK?'

Campbell's warm breath was everything you'd expect from someone who used dried cuttlefish instead of toothpaste. 'You need to slow down, Jessica. You'll never appreciate natural beauty if your head's still walking around T K Maxx.'

'Wish it was,' I said. 'And do you mind not calling me Jessica? It's Jess, yeah?'

'We try not to abbreviate here, *Jessica*,' said Campbell. 'You'll be talking in text speak next!'

I was getting angry now. 'Are you lot for real? I mean, you're not honestly into all this crap?'

'I wouldn't let Derek hear you say that if I were you,' said Campbell. 'He's put his heart and soul into this place – we all have.'

Lucy was staring intently at my clogged pores. 'I know what her trouble is. She's in mourning for her mascara. Poor little girlie can't get to sleep without a full-facial and her digital curling tongs.'

Even the oversized seagulls squealed with laughter. I was just furious that she'd called it so well. 'I can't believe you're actually OK with this. I mean, what do you do all day? How can you live without a phone?'

'Best thing I've ever done,' said Campbell.

'And why do you wet yourselves every time a bird flies past? It's not natural.'

'Little bit of advice, Jessica,' said Lucy. 'If you want to fit in around here, you'd better start showing some respect for our Dawdler ways.'

'What, like you lot, you mean?'

'Yes, that's exactly what I mean,' said Lucy.

But I wasn't finished yet. 'OK, then, tell me this. If meditation is so bloody amazing, why did you all walk out of the Symposium last night?'

Campbell smiled infuriatingly. 'You heard what the man said: it's not compulsory. There are plenty of different ways to meditate, you know.'

'So what were you doing then?'

Campbell didn't answer, but a few seconds later I felt his cold hand on the back of my neck. A quiver of anticipation turned into a shiver of fear when I realised that with one well-timed push he could send me plummeting.

'That's enough, Jessica,' he whispered. 'I think we all know what happens to people who ask too many questions.'

'No, what does happ—'

'OK, everyone, lunch is ready,' called Derek. 'We've got fresh milk and some fennel and goat's cheese sandwiches. Now that's what I call a happy meal.'

'Right, you've had plenty of time to digest your food,' said Derek. 'Before we head back, we really should go down to the beach.'

'Do we have to?' said Campbell.

'Can't we leave it a couple more weeks?' said Lucy.

The other Striplings were equally unenthusiastic. Jack claimed some kind of hamstring injury, the two Harrys preferred to go back via the peat bogs and Molly said she felt sick.

'It's been over two months now,' said Derek. 'Earl says if you don't face up to things, you'll never really be able to move on. In fact, he was down there himself only yesterday morning. Come on, guys; Jessica and I will lead the way.'

There was no running commentary as we descended the twisting, narrow path that led to the beach. I was still confused, and more than a little spooked, by their behaviour on the clifftops, but this brooding silence was even stranger.

Erika and the Junior Laggards were splashing about in a rock pool. They were having such a fun time I felt like kicking off my shoes and joining them. It would have been far more enjoyable than leading a reluctant procession of teenagers across the pebbles to the foot of the cliffs.

'This is it,' said Derek solemnly. 'It's all right, you don't have to come any closer. Maybe you'd like a few moments to yourselves while I have a quick word with Jessica.'

The Striplings huddled together, like funeral guests outside a crematorium. One of the girls appeared to be crying, and I couldn't help noticing that Lucy had slipped her arm around Campbell.

'What's the matter with *them*?' I said.

Derek ushered me out of earshot. 'This is where Earl found Kevin. It's the first time they've been here since the week of the accident. It's no wonder they're upset.'

I forced my head backwards and squinted up at the cliffs. 'How did it happen, Derek? What was he doing up there?'

'You see that rock – the one jutting out about halfway up?'

I felt dizzy just looking at it. 'You mean the one a bit like a sausage?'

'They called it Death Rock,' said Derek. 'If a young crofter wanted to prove himself suitably virile for marriage, he had to climb up to it and steal a fulmar's egg.'

'What's that got to do with Kevin?'

Derek dabbed his eyes with an unpleasant-looking handkerchief. 'He was trying to recreate it, you see – the old crofter ritual. Must have lost his footing; poor lad didn't stand a chance.'

'Can we go now, please?' called Campbell, sounding more

like a frightened kid than the prototype Bond villain on the clifftop.

'Yes, of course,' said Derek. 'And well done, guys. I'm really proud of you.'

No one said much on the way back. Even the sight of a flock of cackling kittiwakes merited little more than a polite gasp. It was only when we arrived back at the Symposium that the Striplings started reverting to their disgustingly animated selves.

'Thank you, Derek. Those fulmars were awesome.'

'Wasn't the light sensational?'

'I'm going to write a poem about a Viking warrior seeing the island for the very first time.'

'Yes, well, don't work too hard,' said Derek. 'You know what the afternoons are for.'

They turned, like a well drilled, but appallingly styled, dance troupe. A moment later the Striplings were gone.

'Where are they off to?' I said.

'To the new forest,' said Derek. 'The afternoons are set aside for free play. Did you know that according to a recent study, you guys are the unhappiest young people in Europe? You grow up so fast you don't have time to be just children any more. We want our Striplings to experience some of the innocent pleasures that twenty-first-century living has denied them: playing in the woods, building dens, climbing trees . . . getting their knees dirty.'

Never mind compulsory euthanasia and genetic engineering, the thought of hanging out in the woods with the Striplings sounded about as dystopian as it gets.

'Let me tell you something, Jessica: nothing gives me more

satisfaction than the sound of their infectious laughter.'

'Should I go with them?' I said, doubtfully.

'Not today. There's something I need to show you first.'

The Dawdler library was a medium-sized pod a short walk from the composting toilets. 'They're shutting these places down on the mainland,' said Derek, stepping through the entrance hatch and clicking on the light. 'We really are very lucky.'

At least our local library, which I'd visited more regularly since the skinny-jeaned Adonis from Millie's debating society started his Saturday job, had a couple of past it computers and a selection of DVDs. The Dawdler version was just a couple of rickety shelves and some smelly books.

'That's the Young Adult section,' said Derek. 'Why don't you go and chose one?'

'Only *one*?' You could take twenty books and as many DVDs as you wanted from the place in town.

'We prefer you to concentrate on one thing at a time,' said Derek. 'Now tell me, what sort of fiction are you really passionate about?'

Despite what I might have suggested to skinny jeans boy, the only book I'd read lately was a synopsis of *Lord of the Flies*. Luckily, Millie wasted hours with her head in a paperback. At least I knew what *she* was passionate about. 'Have you got one about a dying teenager who wants to have sex?'

Derek winced. 'I don't think so, Jessica. But I'm sure you'll find something much more suitable. What we have here are timeless classics.'

Never mind judging a book by its cover, the titles said it all. *Little Lord Fauntleroy* sounded almost as ridiculous as *Swallows and Amazons* and who gave a toss about *What Katy Did*? *Black Beauty* was about a horse who wasn't even a private detective, *The Secret Garden* should probably have stayed that way and if *Tom Brown's Schooldays* were anything like mine, it would have been a total waste of time writing a book about them.

'Thanks, I'll have this one,' I said, pulling out a battered hardback with a picture of a tunnel on the front. 'Do I have to get it stamped or something?'

'We operate on trust here,' said Derek. 'Good choice, I see.'

Mum made us watch it on telly every Christmas. And every year she cried at the end when the kids' dad got off the train. *The Railway Children* was a disgustingly syrupy movie, but at least I'd be able to blag it if he started asking questions.

'I'll see you at dinner, then,' said Derek, waving me out into the light. 'The new forest's that way, Jessica. Why don't you go and join the Striplings? I'm sure they'd be delighted to see you. Or perhaps you just want to get stuck into your new book.'

I had no intention of doing either, but just to pacify him I glanced at the back cover of *The Railway Children* before taking a few paces towards the new forest and listening for the for the sound of infectious laughter.

But I didn't hear any.

Stormy Weather

That night there was the mother of all storms. Earl had predicted as much in the Symposium. After such a bright day, it sounded rather unlikely. But the Dawdlers never doubted him, and there was no shortage of volunteers to walk down to the landing stage and fill the fishing boat with rocks. Earl was expecting winds of over one hundred and fifty miles an hour, and if we wanted to keep enjoying all that 'delicious' seafood, it was crucial to stop it blowing away.

They were all so eager to please him, hanging on his every word like he was some kind of prophet or the lead singer in a really credible band. He seemed to have an almost magical ability to make people feel that he cared about them. After meditation, everyone wanted a piece of him. Helga and Toby were desperate to discuss the harvest, a beaky woman in a floral headscarf called Kirsten had an idea for a folk opera and a group of young mums were keen to canvass his opinion on controlled crying (Earl was not a fan), but he still found time to ask if I was having a good time.

It was a pity the Striplings weren't so welcoming. The truth is I was having a terrible time. Millie went off with Sue to collect cowrie shells, so I'd spent the afternoon watching Erika and the Junior Laggards playing skipping games and checked out the dismal shower facilities. I couldn't even text Ella. She could be pretty annoying at times, not to mention her rubbish taste in music, but that didn't stop me missing her. I was so bored I actually started reading *The Railway Children*.

In fact, I was genuinely relieved when Mum said we should all get an early night. And I'd just started dreaming about Dad – a warm comforting dream where he turned up on the island in the speedboat from Brighton pier with fifty-seven varieties of moisturiser and my favourite curling tongs – when the rain started pummelling on the roof.

Earl's weather forecast was spot on. Although to call it a storm was the understatement of the century. It was more like something out of the Bible or a 3D disaster movie. I'd never been frightened of the wind before, but the howling beast that threatened to rip our little pod from the ground and spit it out into the sea was louder than the deafening surround sound at the multiplex. Even the rats scratched restlessly against the walls. Perhaps they were trying to desert the sinking ship. I just hoped they didn't decide to take the short cut across my face.

At first, I wanted to crawl down the connecting tube and wake Mum, but she was so exhausted after her first day in the health centre that I didn't dare. According to her, the Dawdlers were even worse hypochondriacs than 'real people'.

If only Dad had been there too, I wouldn't have felt half so scared. Except he wasn't, so I cowered beneath the itchy blankets, praying it would soon pass over. But when the wind forced its way through the tiny porthole in the ceiling, freezing my face with its icy breath, I knew the storm was getting closer.

I had a special night-time playlist for just such an emergency. But without my iPod, there was no wall of sound to hide behind, no comforting favourites to mask my feelings of helplessness and muffle my fears. If ever I needed an older sister, it was now.

I stumbled across to Millie's futon, tapping her gently on the shoulder before resorting to a vigorous poke in the ribs. 'Mills, wake up. I need to talk to you.'

She whispered a drowsy expletive and wrenched open her eyes. 'What do *you* want?'

'I need to ask you something.'

'What about?'

'You *know* what about. Come on, Millie, surely you can tell me now. What's the deal with you and Mum?'

'Do you mind? I'm trying to sleep. Sue's giving me my first carving lesson tomorrow. I don't want to be tired.'

'Why are you acting so weird?'

'You'd be acting weird if someone started giving you the third-degree in the middle of the night. Just go back to sleep, why don't you?'

'Please, Mills, *talk to me*. If you're hiding something, I want to know.'

Millie reached out instinctively and touched my cheek.

'Please, Jess, just go back to sleep. There's nothing to tell.'

'But I . . .'

She turned her back on me, rolling into a tight ball like a harassed hedgehog. 'And stop making such a bloody fuss.'

By now I was shaking like the walls of the pod. It was dark, I was terrified, and it felt like the wind was out to get me. The more it howled, the more I missed my music and the more I missed my friends. But more than anything, I missed my family. With Dad over five hundred miles away, and Mum and Millie so distant they might as well have been in China, I'd never felt more alone.

What Jessica Did Next

A week later, things were no better. Dinner was over, but before meditation, Kirsten was leading a music appreciation session. The last thing I needed was a dose of ancient music played on an ancient wind-up gramophone.

'Does this sound familiar?' said Kirsten, cranking the handle. 'Twenty thousand songs to choose from and not one that you've listened to the whole way through? That's why, for the next six weeks, we'll be concentrating on Alfred Cortot's classic 1929 recording of Chopin's waltz in C sharp minor (opus 64 number 2).'

'What, every night for six weeks?' whispered Mum. 'She's got to be joking.'

'There's too much choice these days,' said Sue. 'Earl says

114

that channel hopping is almost as stressful as a messy divorce.'

'You brought us here,' said Millie. 'It's not our fault if you can't handle it. What's the point, anyway? Why can't we just get on with meditation?'

I thought by now they would have made up, but the tension between Mum and Millie was getting worse. Neither of them would tell me what it was all about, and I'd almost given up asking. Whatever it was, they both looked pretty damned miserable.

Millie claimed to be helping with Kevin's memorial, but Sue said she hardly ever turned up to their carving sessions. I was worried about her. The one thing she seemed to look forward to was meditation. I had a feeling it was her way of trying to escape.

And Mum was just as bad. She'd already stopped changing for dinner, and her spirits were fading faster than her scruffy jogging pants. All she ever talked about was work, and how impossible it was when 'our beloved leader' kept interfering. According to Earl, the best cure for everything from constipation to chicken pox was 'a lethal dose of aquatic bog beans'.

It felt like they were slowly slipping away from me, and I missed them both.

Kirsten placed the record on the turntable and lifted the needle. 'Now, first time through, I think you should just try and listen for the arpeggio figures in the left hand.'

Alfred Cortot's legendary 1929 recording of Chopin's waltz in C sharp minor (opus 64 number 2) sounded rather like having your tooth drilled while someone played the piano in a distant waiting room. I got to know it pretty well over the next few weeks, but that first time, I didn't even notice the 'subtle tempo change' in the second section; I was far too preoccupied with what I'd decided to do next.

I was lonely. And in some strange way I think I was actually missing school. St Thomas's could be terrible at times, but at least if you were enduring the wind band's latest rendition of 'The Circle of Life' or stuck in detention, there was always someone your own age to share the pain with. I suppose that's why I kind of started obsessing about the Striplings. Our mornings with Derek were a grim mixture of pointless discussions and hard labour. When we weren't trudging round the island in search of endangered species, Derek shared his thoughts on advertising or genetic engineering while we humped wheelbarrows of manure to the allotments or mucked out the pigs.

But there was something about the Striplings that didn't quite add up. I mean what were the odds of eight teenagers getting so hyped about natural fence weaving techniques? That's why I started watching them. If anyone was faking it, sooner or later they'd have to let something slip.

I even pretended to be having a good time, eagerly volunteering for some of the worst jobs in history and flashing my fake smile until my face ached. That way they wouldn't suspect. In fact, I got so good at it that an innocent bystander would probably have believed that globalisation and pig shit were just about my favourite subjects. And although they never once invited me to their afternoons of riotous free play (the idea of getting my knees dirty in the woods was totally disgusting anyway), I was pretty confident that the Striplings believed it too.

The trouble was the Striplings *never* slipped up. They sat entranced through Derek's talk on environmental degradation and joined in the discussion afterwards like guest nerds on a late-night telly show. Admittedly the seals on the north beach were kind of cute, but all they wanted to talk about was their 'complex courtship rituals', and how Edward was working on an in-depth study.

And Campbell was the king of the eco-freaks. He was always ready with a smartarse answer, and the way he kept disappearing into whispery huddles with Lucy was truly nauseating. I watched him closer than anyone.

But if I really wanted to test my theory, my best chance was to catch them unawares. What were they like when they knew I wasn't watching them? It wasn't much of a plan, but it was all I had. Every night they'd slipped out of the Symposium before meditation. This time, I'd decided to follow.

I was desperate to get on with it, but Earl was angry that night. After the sixth and final dose of Chopin, he jumped onto the stage and ranted for a good twenty minutes. I'd never seen him like that before. His cheeks glowed unhealthily and the teeth he usually flashed at every opportunity were kept carefully hidden behind closed jaws. They were grown adults, but by the time he'd finished with them, the Dawdlers looked like a shell-shocked group of Year Sevens after Mr Catchpole's annual 'mindless vandalism' lecture.

'All right, that's enough from me,' said Earl, snapping his fingers at the guys with the candle. 'All I'm saying is that we can't possibly call ourselves hunter-gatherers if so few of us are prepared to slaughter our own food.' He stared accusingly at his flock. 'OK, let's make this a good one, shall we?'

Campbell and the others had left the Symposium. Millie was staring fixedly at the candle and Mum was so knackered I don't think she even heard me when I whispered, 'Just popping out for a bit,' and drifted slowly towards the entry hatch.

Earl had got it right again; summer really *was* on its way. The stars were splashed across the sky like spilled milk and the lingering sunset was bathing the moor in a golden haze. OK, that sounds weird, doesn't it? Twinkling stars and golden sunsets aren't really my thing, but it felt so good to be outside in just my jumper, jeans and thickest hoodie. As for the stars, I had this silly idea that Dad might be watching them too. Well, there wasn't much else to do at Grandma's – unless you were addicted to Scrabble and Rich Tea biscuits. Two days at Christmas was bad enough, but by now he'd be climbing up the walls.

And then I remembered the reason I was out there in the first place. They were running up the side of the hill in a squiggly line. The sight of Dawdlers running was one thing, but what really threw me was the alien sound they were making.

It was the sound of infectious laughter.

I'd never heard them laugh like that before. They'd chuckled politely at Derek's pathetic jokes, but this was so carefree, I didn't like the sound of it at all.

But no amount of creepy hilarity could stop me now. It was a steep climb to the top of the hill and the stone circle beyond. Gulping down a mouthful of salty air, I set my sights on the summit and started the ascent.

Every now and then I'd duck down behind a boulder or lie

motionless in the damp heather. That must have been how I lost sight of them. One moment they were laughing their heads off, and the next minute they'd vanished. All I could see was an empty expanse of soggy moorland and the stone circle looming up ahead.

I dawdled aimlessly from stone to stone, exchanging doleful high fives with the cold granite. The scene was eerie enough without the stark wooden cross in their midst. According to Sue, Earl had sobbed uncontrollably as he hammered it into the ground.

'It's OK, Kevin,' I whispered, trying to raise my own spirits as much as his. 'I know what I'm doing.'

But I wasn't fooling anyone. I couldn't even follow a bunch of stupid teenagers up a stupid hill. Out on the rocks, the seals were singing a soulful ballad about a stupid girl with stupid hair who couldn't even follow a bunch of stupid teenagers up a stupid hill. And if the stupid girl wasn't very careful, she'd soon be giving the moon the satisfaction of seeing her cry.

What would Dad have done? Dad was a realist. He wasn't the kind of parent who kept on about how you could do anything you liked if you wanted it badly enough. He'd probably have magicked me up a mug of hot chocolate (with little marshmallows on top) and sent me back to bed. And that's where I was heading, until a pin-prick of light emerged from the old blackhouse on the side of the hill.

'Oh shit.'

I'd deliberately avoided that place. There were gaping sockets where the windows should have been, half the roof was missing, and the weather-beaten walls looked set to collapse at any minute.

Maybe it was just a trick of the light. Yeah, that was it. Sloth was like that. I was probably just seeing things. Much better to pack it in for the night and come back tomo—

AND THERE IT WAS AGAIN.

Unmistakable this time, it winked at me from the window, almost as if the wiley old ruin was sizing up its prey.

Dropping onto my belly and clawing my way across the ground with my forearms, I stalked the old blackhouse like a professional assassin. Perhaps six long weeks with Dan Lulham hadn't been completely pointless after all. How many times had I seen his pathetic mini-me performing exactly the same manoeuvre in that sad killing game he played twenty-four/seven on his Xbox?

Voices; I was sure I heard voices. If I could just get a little closer, I might be able to hear what they were saying. The rear wall was a short crawl through a natural assault course of long grass and nettles. I stretched my sleeves to protect my hands, whispered a soothing mantra of St Thomas's Community College's favourite expletives, and went for it.

Maybe I'd imagined the voices too. Crouching beneath the rear window, all I could hear was my heart beating dubstep and the agonised wheeze of my heavy breathing. Down in the valley, the pods glimmered like a distant family of breast-shaped nightlights. You have no idea how much I wanted to run towards them. But there was nothing for it but to take a peep inside.

The window was right above me. How hard could it be? I turned to face the wall, kneeling in front of the decaying masonry, like I was praying – which is pretty much exactly what I was doing, as I rose slowly to my feet.

'Keep calm and carry on,' I whispered, only centimetres now from the window ledge. It's funny how a few silly words can make you feel better. Because whatever I was about to see, suddenly I was ready for it. Simple really; just straighten my legs and . . .

BLACKNESS! DEEP, DARK AND INPENETRABLE, LIKE I'D SUDDENLY GONE BLIND.

I tried to scream, but it came out all muffled.

'Keep quiet, Jess,' said the voice. 'Someone might hear you.'

I tried struggling, but it was no use. A clutch of hands tightened simultaneously around my arms and neck and dragged me backwards through the nettles.

'Stop kicking, Jess,' said the voice, 'or do you *want* to get hurt?'

They bundled me into the blackhouse, forcing me down onto the dank grassy floor.

'You can let her go now,' said the voice. 'And you'd better take that blindfold off too.'

More hands on the back of my neck. The darkness turned to blinding light.

I was almost too angry to be scared. 'Well, go on, then, big shot; do your worst. What is it that you lot get up to, anyway?'

I couldn't see him because he was shining a torch in my face. But I'd known his voice all along.

'We're the Firewallers,' said Campbell.

Firewallers

Some of the others produced torches too, holding them under their chins, like a low a budget horror movie.

'Hi, Jess,' said Lucy. 'We hoped you'd come.'

'What are you talking about?' I said. 'And what's with the Jess all of a sudden? I thought you freaks didn't abbreviate.'

They all seemed to find that pretty funny.

'I was quite pleased with that one.' Campbell smiled. 'Not bad for the spur of the moment.'

'Oi, Jess,' said the boy in the logo-less baseball cap. 'Why didn't you bring your sister? She's well hot.'

'Don't worry about him, he's got sex on the brain, haven't you, Ed?' said Lucy. 'But is she all right, though? Your sister, I mean. She looked a bit under it.'

'I don't know what's the matter with her,' I said. 'She's been acting all weird since we got here.'

'It takes people that way sometimes,' said Campbell. 'You should have seen some of this lot when they first arrived.'

Naseeb was carrying one of those old-fashioned egg timers, which she kept turning over every time the sand ran out. 'You never really get used to it. You just learn to cope with things.'

I couldn't believe I hadn't clocked it before. All the girls had put their hair up – which was a one million per cent improvement, let me tell you.

'Wait a minute,' I said, starting to wonder if that was really Lucy's natural colour. 'I thought you lot were really into that Dawdlers stuff.'

'That's what we want them to think,' said Ed.

It was more confusing than the Demon Headmaster's uniform policy. 'Are you saying you don't actually like it here?'

'What do *you* reckon?' said Ed.

'It totally sucks,' said Lucy. 'They've had their lives; why do they want to go and ruin ours too?'

'Don't you just hate all that mud?' said Naseeb. 'Never mind those disgusting animals – talk about gross.'

Ed was head-banging in agreement. 'If I never see another "breathtaking sunset" for the rest of my life, it'll be far too soon.'

'Hang on,' I said. 'If you all hate it so much, why don't you tell them?'

'To keep them off our backs,' said Jack. 'It was bad enough when they could only Facebook-stalk you from work. Think what it could be like now they're practically living on top of us.'

'So long as they think we're happy little Striplings, they'll leave us to get on with it,' said Lucy.

'And they really believe you're happy?'

'It's what they want to believe,' said Campbell. 'They're too busy with their tragic mid-life crises anyway.'

'Yeah, right,' said Ed. 'It wasn't the internet that killed childhood, I'll tell you that for a start.'

It still didn't explain why they'd had to scare me silly. 'OK fine, but you could have told me.'

'We had to make sure you felt the same way first,' said Lucy.

'How do you know that I do?'

The blackhouse rocked with uninhibited laughter.

'Oh please,' said Lucy. 'If you really want to look like you're interested in conservation, you'll have to get a lot better at disguising your yawning.'

'Yeah, and real animal lovers don't hold their noses every time they go near one,' added Campbell.

'So how about this . . . Firewallers thing?' I said, anxious not to dwell on my obvious inadequacies as a counterfeit Stripling. 'What's that all about?'

Campbell stepped into the torchlight. 'It's what we do to remember. Each one of us is an expert in some aspect of our old lives.'

Lucy sounded like an annoying co-presenter on the Shopping Channel. 'For instance, Molly's our reality telly person, Ed's our Xbox guy and Naseeb knows everything there is to know about social networking.'

'Yeah, and porn star poses!' quipped Ed.

'We take it in turns to give lectures or run workshops on our specialist subjects,' said Campbell. 'That way we won't forget.'

'How about you, Jess?' said Naseeb. 'What are you an expert on?'

'Dunno. Hair and beauty, I suppose.'

'*I'm* hair and beauty,' said Lucy firmly. 'But I'm sure there's something else you're good at.'

Ed's machine-gun snigger was reassuringly St Thomas's-like.

Naseeb was checking her egg timer. 'We'd better get going. If we stay out too long they'll start asking questions.'

The girls started letting down their hair.

'Wait a minute,' said one of the Harrys. 'Shouldn't someone tell Jess about her initiation?'

'My *what*?'

Campbell smiled sadistically. 'We'll do it tomorrow night, Jess. Same time, same place.'

'Don't worry,' whispered Lucy. 'I'm really girlie and I managed it.'

'But what is it?' I said. 'Tell me about it now.'

The torches went out in unison. A sliver of starlight pierced the hole in the roof.

Campbell was already halfway through the door. 'We haven't got time. And anyway, it's supposed to be a surprise. Come on. Last one to the Symposium has to ask Derek about the ice caps.'

It was the best I'd felt in a long time. Flying down the hill with the Firewallers was the perfect antidote to the worst two weeks of my life. For five minutes at least, the past and the future didn't matter. I wasn't worrying about Dad for a change, or why Mum and Millie seemed to be at war. I wasn't even worrying about the precise details of my so-called initiation. For five minutes at least, I was 'in the moment'.

Campbell was the fastest. He stood outside the Symposium with a smug smile on his face, holding the entry hatch for the rest of us. 'What kept you?' he said. 'Admiring the sunset, I suppose.'

I'd already slowed my pace to a gentle dawdle, realising that if I rolled in last, we could have some one-on-one time. I'm not sure what it was about him, but he needed taking down a peg or two.

'Hey, Campbell,' I said, doing that thing Ella taught me where you suck your cheeks in to make dimples. 'Who made the name up, then? Firewallers, I mean?'

'That would be me,' he said, looking dead pleased with himself.

'Bit lame, isn't it? I mean, what are you, nine years old or something?'

He tried to smile, but what came out was a pleasing mixture of surprise and indignation. 'Well, if you can think of anything better, be my guest.'

'Might just do that,' I said, slipping into the Symposium with a real spring in my step.

Girl Talk

Meanwhile, back at the pod, the past and future were lying wait for me.

'No one dies in it you know, Millie.'

My sister was sitting up in bed, the tatty copy of *The Railway Children* about five centimetres from her face in the solar-powered murkiness.

'And I don't think there's any sex.'

Mum was asleep already. I was still pretty pumped after my encounter with the Firewallers. It was the perfect opportunity to have another go at her.

'You're not still wearing that old sweatshirt are you, Mills?'

Her eyes never once left the page.

'So, what have you been up to all day?'

Millie threw down her book and snarled. 'What are you, my mother or something?'

'No. I just wondered how you were.'

'What do you care? I thought you were too busy saving the world with the Secret Seven.'

I wanted to tell her everything, but I wasn't sure I could trust her not to shoot her mouth off. 'Why don't you come with us tomorrow? They're actually pretty OK when you get to know them.'

'I'd rather stick pins in my eyes.' They were so red and puffy, it looked like she already had. 'Anyway, if you must know, I've been working on my first carving.'

'That's great,' I said, doubtfully. 'When can I have a look?'

'I've only just started,' she said, pulling the blankets around her like a witch's cloak. 'I'm not showing anyone until I'm good and ready.'

That sounded more like the Golden One. She never went public with something until it was absolutely perfect.

'OK, fine,' I said, 'but I want to be the first one to see it when you've finished.'

Millie grunted and buried her head in her pillow. 'Now would you mind switching the light off? I need to get some sleep.'

'OK . . . Night, then . . . See you in the morning . . . Don't let the bed bu—'

'Just get on with it.'

Darkness. Slipping into bed and pulling the coarse grey blanket up to my chin, I remembered that silly joke Dad told us when we were little.

Where were Jess and Millie when the lights went out?

In the dark!

But it wasn't the darkness exactly; it was what you saw in the shadows when your eyes started getting used to it. Two weeks with the Dawdlers and I'd already got part of my childhood back: the terrible feeling that often ambushed me at bedtimes – the feeling that some word-defying catastrophe was about to happen and that I'd be powerless to stop it.

'Millie?'

'*What?*'

'When do you think we'll be going home?'

'How should I know?'

'What's the matter with you? Why are you being like this?'

No answer; just a thousand more questions rising up out of the shadows.

'Mills?'

'What?'

'Do you think . . . Do you think Dad's OK?'

This time she flashed back her answer at the speed of light. 'I don't know and I don't care.'

'Look, I know you hate being here,' I said, trying not to be angry with her, 'but you can't blame Dad, Millie. It's not his fault.'

'How do *you* know?'

'What's that supposed to mean?'

'If you knew what I knew, you might not —'

'Tell me,' I shouted, failing miserably on the anger management front. 'Why are you being such a grade-one bitch?'

'Forget it; doesn't matter.'

'Well, if *you* won't tell me, I'm going to ask Mum.'

Three seconds later Millie was sitting on my futon, her sour breath in my face. 'Don't, please. She's got enough to worry about already. And anyway there's nothing to tell, promise. I'm just a bit . . .'

'Yeah, I know,' I said, a little disappointed that she was already returning to her own bed. 'Hey, Mills?'

'What is it now?'

I thought if I could just cheer her up, she might start seeing things more clearly. 'Can you imagine what a laugh this would be if Dad was here? What do you reckon he'd say if Sue asked him to hand over his laptop? Yeah, exactly. And how do you think he'd cope with meditation?' I gave her a few seconds to enjoy the unlikely image. 'You miss him as much as I do, don't you?'

But I think she was already asleep.

A Very
Respectable Cacophony

'It had better not be goat's cheese again,' said Jack. 'I mean, what exactly is wrong with a burger anyway? No wonder Derek's got the runs.'

'Or even a sub,' said Ed. 'They're supposed to be really healthy.'

Molly was already developing a limp. 'And why do we have to walk everywhere? My feet are nearly as bad as Ed's face.'

Poor Ed could certainly have benefited from a purification mask and a decent defence lotion, but that didn't stop me laughing with the others.

'The whole place is a health and safety nightmare,' said Harry M. Or was it Harry W? 'I'm covered in bites.'

We were trailing up the side of the hill again. Derek was

'indisposed' that morning, so Earl was leading the Striplings to the moor for a 'special workshop'. For someone who believed that speed was the enemy, he certainly looked like a man in a hurry.

'God that bloke's an idiot,' said Jack.

'Give him a break,' said Lucy. 'He's not *that* bad.'

'You obviously haven't heard the latest then,' said Jack. 'He wants to release a pig into the new forest and take the men hunting.'

'That's well cruel,' said Naseeb.

I couldn't help wondering if anyone else had noticed. 'Look, I'm not being funny or anything, but do you think Earl's started wearing make-up?'

'That's what I thought,' said Molly. 'You mean the little black squiggles under his eyes?'

It was good to feel part of something again. Most of them had already popped over to say hi. They'd been on the island since before Christmas ('Worst present ever,' according to Molly) so they were desperate for news from the outside world. I did my best to satisfy them. Jack was keen to pick my brains on the new breakfast menu at Burger King, Harry M wondered if they'd released any more trailers for the *Bond* movie, Naseeb hoped they hadn't been messing about with the Facebook news feed settings again, Molly seemed pleased about the new housemates in *Celebrity Big Brother*, Ed was praying they'd brought zombies back in the latest version of *Call of Duty*, and Harry W was keen to establish if some rapper I'd never heard of had dropped a new mix tape.

But whenever I asked them about my initiation, they smiled mysteriously and reassured me that 'even though I was a girl', I'd probably be all right. All I could think about was Death Rock and those dizzying cliffs. Surely they weren't expecting me to —

'Come on, guys,' called Earl. 'We haven't got all day, you know.'

'I thought that was the whole point,' whispered Harry M.

And then there was Campbell. I had a feeling I'd upset him with my Firewallers joke. It's true he'd sidled up to me outside the Symposium and mumbled a half-hearted apology for 'giving me a hard time', but it wasn't long before he and Lucy were smiling and whispering together, like a celebrity couple on a photo shoot. I didn't know what he saw in her anyway. Her nose was about two sizes too big for her face and that voice of hers was so grating you could make cheese sauce with it.

'OK, guys, gather round,' said Earl. 'Now today I want to show you a very simple technique that will serve you well for the rest of your lives.'

Ed turned and rolled his eyes at me. Jack screwed his index finger into the side of his head.

'Now, I know you Striplings are pretty chilled, but you wouldn't be human if you didn't get angry from time to time.'

'You can say that again,' murmured Harry M.

Earl's designer stubble was turning into a bushy free for all, and he'd exchanged his smart linen suit for cut-down jeans and a hallucinogenic T-shirt. 'Right, we're all going to sit down in a circle and close our eyes.'

There were several enthusiastic noises: 'Sounds interesting', 'It's just what I needed this morning', 'Thanks for this, Earl', but as soon as he closed his eyes we all started making faces at each other. Apart from Campbell of course, who was still spoilsporting an embarrassed frown.

Earl sounded like the bloke off Mum's 'Believe Yourself Thinner' CD. 'Let's start by taking some slow, deep breaths.'

His heavy breathing was positively disgusting; Ed did a disgusting mime to match.

'You see, guys, there's nothing more catastrophic than repressed anger. The trouble is, when something bad happens, that's exactly what most of us do. It feels like we're protecting ourselves, but believe me, it's the *last* thing we're doing.'

A Mexican wave of repressed hilarity raced round the circle.

'But I'd like to start with an apology,' said Earl. 'Not just on behalf of myself, but on behalf of my whole generation. How did children of the sixties create such a terrible world for our own young people?'

Molly's straight face was looking decidedly curvaceous. 'Don't worry about it. It's great what you're doing for us now.'

Earl's voice dropped a few more semitones. 'OK, I want you all to remember a painful experience from your past; something that happened at school, perhaps – a failed exam or a sarcastic teacher?'

He'd obviously met Mr Catchpole.

'But whatever it might be, try to relive that experience; feel those feelings all over again. And this time, instead of holding on to all that anger, you're going to let it go. That's right: shout, scream, stamp your feet – whatever feels right. OK, in your own time.'

We eyed each other nervously, like boys at a party working up the courage to dance. Finally, Jack weighed in with a high-pitched wailing sound, Molly mewled and the two Harrys howled half-heartedly. It was as if someone had slapped on 'I

Bet You Look Good on the Dance Floor'. Suddenly we were all creating our own variations until between us we'd created a very respectable cacophony.

And one of us was really going for it. Even a trained actor would have found it hard to sustain the impressive combination of tears and groans that was starting to dominate; except somehow it grew in intensity, until the sobbing sounded so realistic the rest of us started dropping out to listen.

But then we saw who it was pounding the earth as he wept, his face contorted into a mask of agony and the little black squiggles beneath his eyes forming salty spiders' webs on his cheeks. I'd never seen a grown man cry before, but I had a feeling that Earl was no stranger to it.

'What do we do now?' whispered one of the Harrys.

We huddled, embarrassed, like distant relatives at a funeral. I remember thinking how typical it was of Campbell to want to play mourner-in-chief. 'It's OK,' he said. 'You lot go back to the pods. I'll stay with him until he calms down.'

'Cheers, Cam,' said Ed, already on his way. 'See you later, yeah?'

The others quickly followed; even Lucy, who offered a few words of encouragement before setting off down the hill.

I still hadn't forgiven him for what happened at the blackhouse, but it didn't seem right to leave him like that.

'I'll wait with you if you like. You don't want to be up here on your own.'

Campbell glanced anxiously at Earl who was rocking back and forth with his head in his hands. 'Thanks, Jess, that's really . . . kind of you. It's probably best if you go with them, though.'

'It's OK, I don't mind.'

Earl was bawling again, a rogue slither of snot dangling from his nose.

'*Please*, Jess. I really don't think we should crowd him.'

'Fine,' I said, getting the message that I was surplus to requirements. 'What's the matter with him anyway?'

'He's still upset about Kevin.'

'Listen, Cam,' I said, test-driving his nickname, and liking the way it sounded. 'It's none of my business, but do you think it might be better if we left him to it?'

Earl began to howl.

'Look, I've told you,' said Campbell. 'I'm just going to make sure he's OK. Now *please* go. If you leave now you'll catch up with the others.'

'Yeah . . . right,' I said, taking a few reluctant steps towards the pods.

'Hey, Jess,' called Campbell.

'Yes.'

He just looked at me. 'Nothing. I'll see you tonight at your initiation.'

Earl must have been riddled with anger. Halfway down the hill I looked back again. He was sobbing uncontrollably, and Campbell was standing over him with his hand on his shoulder.

Hungry
Like The Wolf

'OK, Harry,' said Campbell solemnly. 'Let her have it.'

They trained their torches on a spot halfway up the blackhouse wall. Harry M nodded at Harry W who started removing bricks to create a laptop-sized hole.

'It's not here,' said Harry W, his arm disappearing into the wall like a vet at a calving.

'Let me try,' said Campbell. 'I've got longer arms than you.'

Lucy had insisted on putting my hair up in a messy bun (with a band and some grips from her 'secret store'), so I felt almost human for once. The trouble was I felt suspiciously like a human sacrifice. Just because they'd been nice to me for a few hours didn't mean they couldn't suddenly turn nasty.

'It's not . . . dangerous, is it?' I said, trying not to think of Death Rock.

There was plenty of knowing laughter, but no one answered my question.

'Gotcha!' said Campbell, pulling out a small rectangle of lime green plastic and passing it to Jack.

Harry M held it up to the torchlight. 'Now please be careful, Jess. It's over ten years old.'

'And switch it off as soon as you finish,' said Campbell. 'We're running out of batteries.'

I don't think I'd ever seen one before. It was practically an antique. 'Sorry, I'm a bit confused.'

Harry M cradled it over to me, like a new mother surrendering her baby to an accident-prone aunt. 'The Gameboy Color,' he said. 'Over one hundred million units sold worldwide; fifty-six colours simultaneously from a palette of thirty-two thousand. I picked it up at a car boot sale – couldn't believe my luck. Without this baby we would never have had the Xbox.'

'Yeah, well, that's a matter of opinion,' said Ed.

Harry M didn't rise to the bait. 'Notice the infra-red transfer port. You could actually use that as a TV controller.'

Jack whistled appreciatively.

'Turn it on,' said Harry M. 'You'll find the switch on the right hand side.'

'OK then, but I still don't get it.' A familiar logo flashed onto the screen accompanied by a satisfying electronic beep. '*Rampage – World Tour*. Never heard of it.'

'It's a simple side-scrolling smash 'em up,' said Harry M. 'Set it to difficult and select a monster.'

'So what's it got to do with my initiation?'

'You have three minutes to get forty-five thousand points,' said Campbell. 'Why, what did you expect?' he added smugly.

'I'll help you out if you like, babe,' said Ed, standing behind me and slipping his hands over mine.

'*No thanks*,' I said, removing myself from his sweaty clutches and selecting Ralph the Wolf. 'And I'm not your babe, OK?'

Naseeb was in charge of the egg timer. 'Are you ready, Jess?'

I nodded.

'They all joined in with the countdown. 'Five, four, three, two, one . . . GO!'

I wasn't a complete noob. I'm not exactly proud of this, but I was part of the Pokémon craze that swept Warmdene Primary in Year Five, so I knew my way around a Gameboy Advance. How different could it be?

And it kind of reminded me of those epic battles with 'the elite four'; everyone crowding round to get a better view of the screen and offering words of advice.

'Watch out for the helicopters.'

'If you punch out the windows, the buildings just collapse on themselves.'

'You can get more health by eating people.'

The instructions said, *Destroy all buildings to advance to the next city.* But the graphics were terrible and it wasn't nearly as easy as it looked.

'Two minutes to go,' said Naseeb. 'Come on, Jess; you've got to smash them!'

Everyone groaned when my wolf died. 'Noooooooahhhhhh!'

By the end of the first level I was only on five thousand,

four hundred points. 'I don't think I can do this.'

'Course you can,' said Campbell. 'Press *Start* to continue.'

The buildings in level two (Liverpool) were taller and there were loads more people about. Once I'd eaten a few, I actually started enjoying myself.

'Last thirty seconds,' said Naseeb. 'Come on, Jess, you can do it.'

I reached Kankakee on thirty-seven thousand. By now I was sensing the hazards before they even arrived, zapping the skyscrapers for fun.

'Five . . . Four . . . Three . . . Two . . . ONE!'

'*Yesss*!' I screamed, punching the air before joining the rest of them in an orgy of high-fiving.

'Forty-six thousand, five hundred,' said Harry M, snatching back his precious baby and flicking off the switch. 'Not bad, I suppose, but it won't exactly put you on the leader board.'

'Well done,' said Lucy, giving me a little hug. 'Your hair looks good too, Jess.'

'Thanks.'

'Well, I suppose you can call yourself a Firewaller now,' said Campbell, making to hug me, but opting at the last minute for a pat on the shoulders. 'That's if you haven't thought of a better name!'

'Hey, Jess,' said Molly. 'What's your specialist subject then?'

With hair and beauty taken there was only one option. 'Epic fail videos.'

'What, like the bald bloke treading grapes?'

'That's right.'

'I'll schedule in a presentation for next week,' said Naseeb.

'Sweet,' said Harry M. 'I reckon Kev would have loved that.'

'*Really?*' I said. 'I didn't think he'd be particularly into it.'

'What makes you say that?' said Lucy.

'I kind of got the impression he was more interested in all the Dawdler stuff. Isn't that why he wanted to climb up to Death Rock?'

'Kevin hated it more than any of us,' said Ed. 'He was just better at hiding it.'

Harry M gleamed angrily in the torchlight. 'I still don't buy that crofter rubbish. Kev couldn't give a stuff about it. And you know what he felt about physical exercise.'

'We've been through all this before,' said Campbell. 'Why can't you just let him rest in peace?'

'I just don't get it,' said Harry M. 'All he really cared about was MMORPGs.'

'Massively multiplayer online role playing games,' added Ed – helpfully for once.

Harry obviously wasn't ready to let Kevin rest in peace. 'His user name was Rainbow Warrior. And I don't care what anyone says, he would *never* have tried to recreate some pathetic macho ritual. Kev was a real —'

'Look, we haven't got time for this now,' said Campbell. 'They'll be finishing soon. We need to get back to the Symposium.'

'Yes, come on,' said Lucy. 'Earl might be off his trolley, but he's right about one thing; we all have to move on. Now let's get out of here.'

'Hey, Jess,' whispered Campbell, accidentally brushing my hand as torches were extinguished and we headed for the door. 'Did you ever wonder what we really got up to in our free play sessions? Well, tomorrow afternoon, you're going to find out.'

The Game

'We'll talk some more about Thomas Paine next time,' said Derek, scuttling towards the composting toilets. 'And we'll be cleaning out the chicken house, so don't forget to bring appropriate footwear. Enjoy your free play now.'

'Thanks, Derek, that sounds terrific.' said Lucy, changing her tune the moment he disappeared into the cubicle. 'Oh God, not another morning scraping bird poo. That's the last thing I need.'

'Yeah, never mind the Rights of Man,' said Harry W, 'what about *our* rights?'

Erika and the Junior Laggards were dancing round the totem pole, whooping it up deliriously in stark contrast to our cheerless crocodile of teenage resentment.

But the mood improved as we forged deeper into the new forest. Ed took a vote on our favourite pointless websites (a toss-up between unnecesarilylongurl.com and isitchristmas.com) and Naseeb made everyone update their relationship status. There was some less than polite banter when Ed ('It's complicated') cast aspersions on Jack's claim that he was 'in an open relationship', but for most of us it was just harmless fun. Apart from Campbell of course, who was having none of it:

'What's the point? I'm not even on Facebook any more.'

'Come on, Campbell. Don't be shy,' said Naseeb. 'Is there something, *or someone*, you want tell us about?'

Like it wasn't obvious anyway; if Lucy was 'in a relationship', her victim could hardly be anyone else. I actually felt quite sorry for him. As Mum was always saying, 'The last thing the world needs is another bloke who can't talk about his feelings.'

'Look at his little face,' said Ed. 'Come on, matey, who's the lucky girl?'

Campbell's cheeks were on fire. 'I don't know what you're talking about . . . I mean, even if I did, you know, *like* someone, I wouldn't —'

It was so agonising to watch I thought I'd better change the subject. 'So . . . anyway, guys, what's this big surprise you've been promising me? I suppose you've got a couple of Xboxes stashed away or something.'

'Not quite,' said Campbell, flashing me what looked like a grateful smile. 'What would you *like* it to be, Jess?'

'A half decent nail bar would be nice.'

'You wish,' said Lucy.

'It's better than that,' said Jack. 'Just wait until you see it.'

'It's not a branch of Nandos by any chance?'

'You'll never get it,' said Lucy. 'Put it this way, it's something we can *all* enjoy.'

And I was getting quite excited until we came to a clearing and they all shouted, 'Ta-daa!'

I didn't even bother to disguise my disappointment. 'You have *got* to be joking. What is it anyway?'

'It's our den,' said Campbell apologetically. 'Derek built it. Apparently he spent half his childhood traipsing round the countryside. According to him, he was out in the woods until all hours. Yeah, I know – nightmare.'

It was a disgustingly random combination of oil drums and driftwood that kind of reminded me of the bearded colony of protestors who set up camp outside Dad's bank the previous summer.

'*That's it?*' I said. 'That's the big surprise you've dragged me all the way down to the woods for?'

'Of course not,' said Campbell, peeling back the smelly tarpaulin that covered the entrance. 'Grab yourself a seat and we'll show you.'

No wonder Mum refused to go on camping holidays. At least there were enough holes everywhere to let the sunlight in, but by the time everyone had found a driftwood stool, or if you were lucky, one of those fold-up chairs that old people keep in the car boot, it was sweatier than a seething mosh pit.

'Are you ready for this, Jess?' said Campbell, scrabbling around in a pile of leaves and pulling out a Sainsbury's carrier bag.

'Yeah . . . whatever.'

He lowered the carrier bag into my lap. It was heavier than

I thought. 'Go on; take a look.'

It felt like opening a Christmas present from Dad's aunt in Littlehampton who always sent me and Millie matching scarves. Until I saw what it was. 'It's not, is it?'

Campbell nodded. 'Kevin smuggled it back from the mainland, when he had his tooth out.'

'I love this book,' I said, flicking through the first thousand pages or so until I came to my favourite bit.

'Really brings it back, doesn't it?' said Campbell.

The others had pulled their chairs even closer so they could look over my shoulder and make comments.

'Toni & Guy digital hair straighteners; I've got some of them.'

'Can we see the digital photo frames next?'

'What about those hi-def camcorders where you can upload straight to YouTube?'

I could see now what Lucy meant. There really was something for all of us to enjoy. Never mind the Bible and Shakespeare, or even *The Railway Children* for that matter – the Argos catalogue was perfect desert island reading material.

'Go on, Cam,' said Lucy. 'Tell her about the game.'

Campbell kneeled beside me, his hand centimetres from mine on the plastic armrest. 'OK, Jess, the rules are simple. You've got a grand to spend on anything you like. What do you buy?'

'How long do I have?'

'As long as you like,' said Lucy. 'We all keep changing our minds anyway.'

The rules might have been simple, but it turned out to be the most difficult game I'd ever played. 'Right, I think I might start with a decent hairdryer . . . No wait, how much is the cheapest portable DVD player? And what do you guys think of 3D tel—'

It was the strangest sound I'd ever heard: halfway between a deep-throated roar and a cry for help. But if that wasn't enough to distract me from my catalogue shopping, the rhythmic chanting floating across from another part of the forest was impossible to ignore. 'What is *that*?'

'Haven't you heard?' said Jack. 'Earl reckoned the men were too soft to be hunter-gatherers anyway, so he's started a wrestling club. No one wanted to do it of course, but they haven't got the guts to stand up to him.'

Ed was already doing my head in with his lame American accent. 'The first rule of wrestling club is that you don't talk about wrestling club. The second rule of —'

'My dad reckons he's losing it,' said Molly. 'You saw him the other day. What was he *like*?'

'No offence,' said Harry W, 'but if you ask me the bloke's a complete lunatic.'

'Give it a rest,' snapped Campbell. 'Jess can't concentrate.'

He was absolutely right. But it wasn't the sound of middle-aged men shouting encouragement at their flabby contemporaries that was making the choice between a multi-purpose professional HD projector and a fully-automated bean to cup espresso machine (for Dad) such a difficult one; it was being so close to Campbell that I could almost feel his heartbeat. I knew he was 'in a relationship', but that didn't stop me studying the back of his long, spotty neck, or wondering what he'd do if I was brave enough to lean down and kiss it.

History
Retweets Itself

As the weeks passed, I lost all track of time. It was bad enough living without *The Great British Bake Off* and having to brush my teeth with ground cuttlefish, but the Dawdler existence was so comatose that one day seemed to merge into the next. It was only the regular programme of Firewaller activities that brought some much needed structure into our lives. At night we escaped to the blackhouse where we put our hair up and tried to remember the old days, and in the afternoons we walked out to the new forest for another round of the game or to give presentations on our specialist subjects.

Ed discussed the relative merits of *Battlefield* and *Call of Duty* (OK, I might have drifted off a bit, but I think it was basically a case of *CoD* for single gameplay and *BF* for multiplayer), Molly talked us through an imaginary

PowerPoint she'd devised about her top ten housemates, and Jack shared his passion for Pizza Hut.

Maybe I resented the fact that she and Campbell seemed to be joined at the hip, but Lucy's thoughts on 'problem hair' contained several inaccuracies that I felt compelled to correct. (Tea tree oil does *not* dehydrate the follicles and straighteners are the last thing you need in the war against frizz). As for Campbell, it didn't really surprise me that his specialist subject, Computer Hacking in the Age of the Script Kiddie, was of so little practical use. Even so, I made sure he saw me laughing at his gone phishing joke.

Although I like to think The Epic Success of the Epic Fail Video had something for everybody, and Harry M's take on the Potter franchise certainly sparked some lively debate, it was Harry W's guided meditation that went down best. He must have known Lakeside Shopping Centre like the back of his hand because he guided us all the way from the car park, through most of our favourite shops on the ground floor, not forgetting a circuit of the Apple Store on level two, right up to the food court at the top. Catalogue shopping was one thing; this way we could enjoy every sight, sound and smell.

'OK, so you're at the top of the escalator. Now I want you to breathe in for a count of three. One . . . two . . . three: I love the smell of doughnuts in the morning.'

After a while, I knew everything there was to know about everyone: favourite band, favourite live band, favourite Friend (mostly Joey, but Molly had this weird thing for Gunther, the guy in Central Perk), favourite app (probably Instagram), favourite regular conditioner, favourite bad hair day conditioner – I even knew how many followers they had on Twitter.

But, apart from Ed's comment about his dad's divorce lawyer, no one really talked about their friends and family or why they'd come to the island in the first place. I certainly didn't feel like talking about mine. A month into our stay and Mum was so negative about everything it was almost as if she'd given up on us. She loathed her work at the surgery, and she'd stopped doing all the 'Mum' things, like trying to tell me what to wear, prying into my eating habits and asking me if I'd had a good day, weeks ago. She'd even stopped trying to get through to Millie, and whenever I mentioned Dad she found some lame excuse to dash off to the health centre or the composting toilets.

We occasionally passed Millie on our dreaded nature Dawdles. Head down and hugging herself like she was modelling a straitjacket, she wandered the island with a kind of haunted look on her face. She still claimed to be working on her mystery carving project, but I never saw any sign of it. And she looked such a sight in her baggy black sweatshirt that I was almost ashamed of her.

I tried to lose myself in all the Firewaller stuff, but I was worried sick about both of them. Mum looked like she was on the verge of some kind of breakdown, and Millie just couldn't cope without Dad. But I never told anyone. I was still clinging to the vain hope that it would all work out in the end. After all, that's why Mum had brought us to Sloth in the first place, wasn't it?

And I kind of figured some of the others must have similar stories to tell. After all, you don't drag your family off to a remote Scottish island if your life's as perfect as a toilet-paper commercial. It was only after Naseeb produced a wad of Post-its and a leaky biro and told us to tweet our back-stories that stuff started to come out. And that's when I realised how much I missed it – the special online intimacy, the way you can open up to anyone about anything and really be yourself.

Harry Mattingly @hazzer46
One morning I'm starring in a coming of age rom-com.
2 #badparents later it's a crap disaster movie.

Harry Wells-Thorpe @HarryWells-Thorpe2
Why did they have to tell me in Pizza Express?

Lucy Wickham @becauseImworthit
Happy in Camden falls foul of crazy uncle's vanity project.

Jack Hardy @frieswitheverything
If this is so good for me, how come the only thing I dream about is the sub of the day?

Molly Elizabeth @bigsisteriswatchingyou
Everything was fine until Mum started Zumba.

Naseeb Conway @naseebio
Worst parents in Wimbledon find perfect way to do head girl's head in.

Ed Bradley @urbansexgod
There must have been #fiftywaystoleavemymother. So why did he pick the cruellest one?

Jess Hudson @Jess_H24
How can you be sure that someone you love is really the person you think they are?

Campbell Lee-Alan @Campbell07
Do we have to do this?

Of course the adults didn't have a clue what we were up to. So long as they believed we were happy, they pretty much left us to our own devices. And part of the fun was fooling Derek. One afternoon, we told him we were going down to the landing stage for a swim. According to him, he'd spent entire summers of his glorious childhood on the sands at Littlehampton. We had no intention of doing it of course, we'd just sit on the beach and talk technology. But it was worth it just for the look on Derek's face when Ed said that swimming in the sea would remind us we were servants of the universe, not masters of it.

Everyone thought Campbell was joking at first. We were debating the advantages of the touchscreen, when he started undressing. 'OK, you lot, who's coming for a swim?'

'Yeah, nice one,' said Jack. 'And put your clothes on, there're ladies about.'

'I'm serious,' said Campbell, stepping out of his jeans and laying them carefully on his shoes and socks. 'It's really hot.

How about you, Jess? Fancy a swim?'

I tried hard to keep my eyes above waist level. 'I'm all right, thanks. Salt water's bad for my hair.'

'What's the matter,' said Campbell. 'You lot chicken or something?'

I still don't know who started it (probably one of the Harrys) but pretty soon we were all laughing hysterically, kicking off our trainers and struggling out of our jeans.

Everyone joined hands, and Naseeb started singing the theme tune from *Titanic* as we stepped gingerly across the pebbles towards the clear blue sea.

My God it was cold in there. No one did much swimming, apart from Campbell who breast-stroked like an Olympian, of course. What we *did* have was the most massive water fight. Lucy and the two Harrys pretended to be their favourite *Simpsons* characters, while the rest of us were mutant ninja zombie Tellytubbies. It sounds lame, I know, but it was such a release that I soon forgot about my hair and concentrated on soaking Krustie the Clown.

And you know what? If I ever felt truly happy on the island, it was the afternoon we went swimming.

But the long summer nights were tinged with melancholy. I couldn't put it into words exactly, although somewhere in the back of my mind I think I must have realised that our little oasis of sanity couldn't last forever.

Part Three

Mates, Dates and Eye-gouging

It was the conversation I'd been dreading. Lucy ambushed me outside the composting toilets after meditation.

'Jess! Jess, wait up. I need to talk to you.'

'What is it?' I said, wondering if she knew that I knew that she knew.

'I hear you've got a date with Campbell tonight.'

I'd have been rubbish on that TV show with the lie detector. 'I don't think it's a date exactly. We're just going for a walk.'

'It's a date.' Lucy smiled. 'Trust me. At least, Campbell thinks it is. I hope you're not leading him on or anything.'

'*No* . . . I mean —'

'Good,' said Lucy. 'Campbell's a great guy. I'd hate to see him hurt.'

And now I was confused. When Ollie Bennett dumped Tash Wilson to go out with Ella, it was World War Three and a Half with a few rounds of eye-gouging thrown in. What was Lucy playing at?

'It just happened,' I said, surreptitiously assessing the length of her fingernails. 'I'm really sorry.'

Now it was Lucy's turn to look confused. 'What have you got to be sorry about?'

'You and Campbell. How long were you . . . you know?'

'Eh?'

She obviously wanted me to spell it out for her. 'How long were you and Campbell together?'

Lucy's hand twitched at her side; I flinched as it flew upwards. But it wasn't my face she was aiming for. Even with her hand clamped to her mouth she still couldn't stifle her unladylike laughter. 'Oh my God! You thought that . . .' She seemed to be having difficulty breathing. 'You thought that me and Cam were an item?'

I reviewed the evidence like a plodding equine sleuth. 'Well, you're always hanging out together . . . and whispering and stuff. I just assumed you —'

'Cam's my little cousin,' said Lucy. 'He's been having a really bad time lately. He needed a friend, that's all.'

'What, you mean you lot all knew each before you came here?'

'Not all of us,' said Lucy. 'But Ed and Harry W's parents were old friends from music college and I think Molly's mum landscaped Ed's garden.'

'So you and Campbell, you're not . . . seeing each other?'

'Of *course* not.'

'Well, that's a relief.'

'I mean, Cam's lovely once you get past the spiky adolescent thing, but even if we weren't related, he's *so* not my type.' Lucy lowered her voice to a whisper. 'Anyway, I've got something for you. I thought you might need them for your date tonight.'

She handed me a brown paper bag. I couldn't believe it when I looked inside. 'Wow, that's amazing!'

'Quick, put them in your pocket. That lot would go mental if they found out.'

'Thank you *so* much. Look, are you sure you don't need them?'

'My boyfriend's in Camden,' said Lucy. 'I'm not even sure if I'll ever see him again.' Her face clouded over. 'Hadn't you better go and get ready? I thought you had a hot date.'

'Thanks,' I said, already wondering what top to wear. 'Hey, Lucy?'

'Yes.'

'What did you mean just now when you said Campbell was having a hard time?'

'Don't you know?'

'Know what?'

'Why would you anyway?' Lucy shrugged. 'He doesn't exactly broadcast it to the world.'

'Broadcast what?'

She wasn't doing her hair any favours by tugging at it like it. 'Look, it's not really my place to say, Jess. I'm sure he'll tell you when he's ready. Have a great night, yeah?'

'Thanks, I'll try to.'

'And be careful. Earl's taking the men into the forest for another loony survival exercise. There'll be goons everywhere.'

* * *

Back at the pod, I was thanking my lucky stars that Mum had remembered the strappy black top that went so well with my jeans. Luckily she was in bed already, so I'd be able to make my getaway without an eight-hour lecture on the dangers of underage drinking, a rundown of the ten most embarrassing teenagely-transmitted diseases she'd treated in surgery and the importance of texting my whereabouts every five seconds. At least on the island you didn't have to worry about missing the last bus or not walking home through the park, and you certainly didn't need to keep your phone fully charged.

It was probably no accident that there was a serious dearth of mirrors on Sloth. Luckily, it was something I could do in my sleep. So I laid out Lucy's precious treasures on the chest of drawers, swept back my hair and set to work.

'What the hell are you playing at?' said Millie.

My skin was in such terrible condition I'd have been quite glad if I really *could* jump out of it. 'I thought you were asleep.'

'Well, I'm not.'

'I was just . . .'

'I can see what you're doing,' said Millie, the hint of a smile creeping into her voice for the first time in weeks. 'And you're making a right pig's ear of it.'

'Am I?'

'What are you, a vampire or something? I told you about that last year.'

It reminded me of that film about the cheerleader who came out of a coma. Millie still *looked* like crap; why she insisted on slobbing about in Mum's horrific old sweatshirt when there were a couple of perfectly acceptable T-shirts in her chest of

158

drawers was a mystery, but at least she *sounded* more like her old self.

'There's no mirror, that's all.'

'Give it here,' she said, grabbing the eye-liner pencil before I could do any more damage. 'Where did you get it from, anyway? I thought the big bad chief didn't approve of this sort of thing.'

'You won't tell anyone, will you, Mills?'

'Not if you let me do it properly,' she said, spitting on her sleeve and scrubbing out what I'd done already. 'Anyway, in case you hadn't noticed, I haven't exactly been going out of my way to make friends and influence people.'

She'd bitten my head off the last time I'd asked what was up with her, but it almost felt like an invitation. 'Yeah, about that . . . Do you want to tell me why you're so angry the whole time?'

'Look, keep still, OK? Or do you *want* to look like a clown?'

'No, I just . . .'

When I was little, she spent hours making me up as a princess. She still had the same fierce concentration, the attention to detail that extended even to her use of the mascara brush. 'Who are you meeting anyway? The tall, spotty one with the bum fluff, I suppose.'

How did she do that? Millie always knew who I fancied, sometimes before I even knew myself. 'Maybe.'

'Well, I hope you can trust him.'

'Why would you say that?'

'Blokes,' said Millie, like there was no need for further explanation.

'What about them?'

159

She was already slipping back into her coma. 'You think you know them, but trust me, you really, *really* don't.'

'Is this about the guy from college – the one in the play?'

'I think you'd better go, Jess. You don't want to be late, and . . . well . . . I need to get on with something.'

A strange look flickered across my sister's face. I didn't recognise it at first, but turning to leave, I realised exactly what it was. It was a look of pity.

Only it wasn't for herself, it was for me.

For God's Sake, Just Kiss Me

Life was so much simpler with mobile phones. We'd arranged to meet outside the blackhouse after meditation; that way we were less likely to be spotted. But Campbell hadn't shown up. Would it really have been the end of civilisation as we know it if I'd been able to text him demanding where the **!! he'd got to?

And pretty soon I was catastrophising. What if he wasn't coming? What if it was like one of those high-school movies where the hot guy asks a dorky girl to the prom for a joke? Luckily Lucy was the only one who knew about it. That was the upside to life on Sloth. At least I wouldn't be trending on Twitter already (#uglymuggings) and at least he couldn't send my picture to half the world and his three little cousins – not that I'd be doing any more photoshoots in a hurry.

It was still humiliating. Maybe I wouldn't have to relive the whole thing on YouTube, like that kid they filmed doing the cinnamon challenge on the war graves trip, but it didn't stop me dreaming up a few choice revenges as I paced angrily in the twilight.

'Hi, Jess,' he said, stepping out from behind the blackhouse and kind of hobbling towards me. 'Sorry I'm a bit —'

'What time do you call this? I've been waiting for hours. *Anything* could have happened.' Fortunately, I was far too angry to realise I was turning into my mother.

'I'm sorry. I got . . . held up.'

After the Dan Lulham disaster, I wasn't going to let another idiot make a fool of me. 'Held up's not good enough, Campbell.'

Which was a pity, because he was looking borderline adorable. He'd somehow managed to slick back his hair and although his tight black shirt wasn't ironed exactly, it was a billion times better than that old jumper.

'Please, Jess, just let me explain.'

'Look, forget it. I'm sorry, Campbell, but I just don't need the hassle right now. Let's go back to the pods.' And then I checked out his bottom half. His white trainers were smothered in what looked like organic chocolate and a steaming damp patch was crawling up his leg. 'What happened to you?'

'I got stuck in the mud, didn't I?'

'Oh come off it, Campbell. What kind of a fool do you take me for? Derek's always warning us about the bog.'

'I was looking for something.'

'What was that, then, the Holy Grail?'

He pulled them out from behind his back, like a bad magician at a children's party. 'Not exactly; I thought you might like these.'

It wasn't the greatest trick in the world, but it still left me speechless. No one had ever given me flowers before. (Dan Lulham bought me a Mars Bar once.) I didn't know what to say.

'Bog asphodels,' said Campbell, holding the posy of delicate yellow flowers under my nose. 'The Latin name means "weak bones" because farmers thought they were bad for their sheep.'

'Oh my God, you're not actually interested in that stuff, are you?'

'Of *course* not,' said Campbell. 'But you can't help picking things up, can you?'

He was right there. That Chopin waltz had been running round my head for weeks. 'If you say so.'

'So you don't want them, then?'

'I didn't say that. I just . . .'

'If you put them in water they might perk up a bit.'

I smiled like the Queen as he handed them over. 'Thanks. They're really . . .'

But Campbell had already turned to leave.

'Hang on a minute; where are you going?'

'I thought you said you wanted to head back.'

'Yeah, well, I changed my mind, didn't I? So come on, Cam. Where are you taking me?'

The animals obviously had no difficulty communicating. Their grunts, snuffles and high-pitched chatterings made our own stuttering attempts at conversation all the more obvious.

'Pigs,' said Campbell.

'Eh?'

'Did you know they can make at least twenty different vocal sounds?'

'Is that right?'

It wasn't the greatest chat-up line I'd ever heard, but it was no worse than Dan Lulham's 'Do you want to come upstairs and see my Xbox?'

'They're intelligent too.'

'Who are?'

'Pigs,' said Campbell. 'Some guy even taught them to play computer games.'

If Dan Lulham could complete *Black Ops* in under six weeks, an intelligent pig ought to fly through it. 'Sorry, Campbell, have you got a thing about pigs or something?'

'I kind of like them, if that's what you mean. And I always go and say good night to Winston – especially when there's something on my mind.'

'Who's Winston?'

'My favourite pig,' said Campbell. 'He's the one with the black eye markings.'

It was the last laugh I had in weeks. 'There's a lot I don't know about you, isn't there, Cam? Got any more dark secrets up your sleeve?'

'*No* . . . No, of course not,' he said, glancing down at his muddy trainers. 'Why would you say that?'

'Calm down, only joking.'

So when was he going to make his move? There were only a few centimetres between us, but it might as well have been the Grand Canyon. By the time we were halfway to

Cineworld, Dan Lulham was all over me like icing sugar.

A new and troubling thought popped into my head. What if, 'Do you want to go for a walk with me tomorrow tonight', actually meant 'Do you want to go for a walk with me tomorrow tonight?' Surely he wasn't that devious.

'Campbell?'

'Yes.'

'Do you mind if I ask you something?'

'Yes . . . I mean, no.' He buried his hands in his pockets. 'It depends what you want to ask.'

Mum sometimes bribed me to watch Jane Austen movies with her, but they were so full of characters who couldn't express their feelings that I spent half the time inwardly screaming, 'For God's sake, just tell him/her'. Maybe it was harder than I thought.

'Is this a . . . ? I mean . . .'

He was studying my face as if some enormous zit had erupted.

'What I mean is, Campbell, is this like a proper date?'

'Would you like it to be a "proper" date?'

'Would *you* like it to be a proper date?'

Campbell stared a little harder. 'Are you wearing make-up?'

'Ten out of ten for observation.'

'You look . . . You look really nice,' he said, switching his attention to the path ahead. 'And yes.'

'Yes what?'

'Yes, I would like it to be a proper date.'

'Good,' I said, doing my best not to sound pathetically relieved. 'So would I.'

An orangey glow had appeared in the new forest. Earl was

roaring the men on to new heights of masculinity.

'Health and safety would go mental,' I said. 'What are they doing down there?'

'He said he wanted to show them the secret of fire,' said Campbell grimly.

'He's getting worse, isn't he?'

'Tell me about it,' said Campbell, stepping up the pace, like he was late for a train.

'What's the hurry?'

'We won't be able to hear that lot when we get to the top.'

He was right. The combination of wind, waves and all-night party animals (the delinquent fulmars, a party of sozzled seals on a stag night) practically drowned them out.

'This way,' said Campbell, leading me towards one of the granite boulders that lay strewn along the clifftop. 'We can shelter behind here.'

He stretched out on the soft grass. I lay down next to him, my left hand trailing at my side, so close to him our fingers were almost touching.

His voice was dreamy and strangely breathless. 'Did you know there are over a hundred billion stars in the Milky Way?'

I *so* thought he was going to make his move. 'I suppose this is where you bring all your girls?'

'*No*. I mean, I haven't got any girls. Not that I've never . . .' He squirmed endearingly. 'This is where I come to think.'

'That's a pity,' I said, turning my face towards him and inwardly screaming, 'For God's sake, just kiss me'.

And I swear Campbell's lips were poised to pounce, when the distant sound of men chanting floated up on the breeze, and he pulled away. 'I'm sorry, I —'

'That Earl is *such* an idiot,' I said, furious that his juvenile antics had interrupted our first kiss. 'I mean, he really gets off on it, doesn't he? Never mind meditation, the guy needs a psychiatrist if you ask me.'

Campbell sat up abruptly, pulling his knees to his chest. 'He wasn't always like that.'

'Eh?'

'Believe it or not, he actually used to be a pretty OK dad.'

I kneeled beside him, trying to get my head around what he'd just said. 'Hang on a minute. Are you saying Earl is your dad?'

Campbell nodded.

It was hard to believe it. They were just so different. Apart from the good looks, of course. 'But how . . . I mean, why . . . I mean, you never said.'

'You never asked. And anyway, it's not something I'm particularly proud of right now.'

'So what happened to him?'

Out on the rocks, the seals were singing a love song. Campbell glared disapprovingly.

'Come on, Cam. It can't be that bad.'

'Want to bet?' He threw back his head and laughed, but it wasn't a happy sound. '*Want to bet*; that's pretty funny actually.'

'Stop it, you're scaring me.'

'Dad worked in advertising,' said Campbell, his sad eyes scanning the universe. 'He fell in love with this place after they shot a hairspray advert here. When the island came up for auction, he said he just *had* to have it. But he never intended to live here. Mum hates all that hippy stuff.'

'So why did . . . ?'

Somewhere in the last thirty seconds our hands had crept across the grass and jumped on each other.

'Mum left when it started getting out of control.'

His palm was warm and clammy. 'What did?'

'Dad's online gambling,' said Campbell. 'Poker mainly, but he wasn't fussed in the end. He said it kept him calmer; Mum didn't see it that way.'

'How come you ended up here?'

'Believe it or not, Dad's commune idea actually sounded like it might be just what he needed – no internet and all that. So I said I'd go too.' Campbell's face wasn't exactly screaming 'happy ending'. 'He was all right to start with, but that all changed when Kevin died. Well, you've seen what he's like now.'

I gave his hand what I hoped was a reassuring squeeze, but it came out more like, *You're not wrong there.* 'I suppose he is kind of . . .'

Campbell squeezed back. 'And then I found out . . .'

'Found out what?'

'Nothing, *nothing*, I mean . . . I . . .' He was like the guy who forgot his lines in Millie's play, spouting randomness until he chanced gratefully on the right words. 'I suppose I realised he wasn't the person I thought he was.'

'What do you mean?'

'I don't know. It was, well . . . another side to him that I'd hardly seen before.'

'Sounds like my sister.'

Campbell flashed me a relieved smile. 'Anyway, it's your turn now, Jess. What brought *you* to Devil's Island?'

'It's a long story.'

'That's OK,' said Campbell. 'I'm not going anywhere.'

And very soon we were lying on our backs, our hands entwined, face to face with a hundred billion stars.

'I suppose I should begin with work experience,' I said. 'And guess what? It sucked.'

'Tell me about it,' said Campbell.

So I told him about it; all the way from Dad's shock marriage counselling announcement, right through to our arrival on the island and my sister's confusing character transplant. And talking about it felt so good that I probably touched on details he really didn't need to know about: Steve the IT guy's great taste in music and less than great taste in fiancées, Brian Simkins' thoughts on the future of the banking industry, the service station breakfast menu, even the ferryman's chances of flogging a book about a dead horse. Campbell was a good listener, whispering a supportive 'What a slime-ball' when I told him about Dan Lulham, squeezing my hand when I got to the part about how much I missed Dad.

And after I'd finished, I suppose I was expecting a few comforting words, not an uncomfortable silence. 'Come on, Campbell, say something.'

He let go my hand, pushing himself up until he was sitting cross-legged, his face crinkled in thought. 'Don't you think it was a bit . . . strange?'

'You're telling me,' I said, lining up next to him like a trainee Buddha. 'But which part are you talking about? Millie's non-existent carving project or an IT guy who really wants to be an artist?'

'I'm probably being really stupid here,' said Campbell, 'but

I don't really see why you suddenly took off like that.'

'I told you. That photograph would have been round the whole school by first break.'

Campbell nodded. 'Yeah, I mean, I can totally see why *you* wanted to get away for a bit. But what about your mum? Don't you think she'd want to stick around to support your dad?'

I'd been thinking up excuses for her ever since we arrived. Now it was time to try them out on Campbell. 'Maybe they needed some time apart. They weren't exactly getting on.'

'So what?' said Campbell. 'You should have seen some of the crap my mum put up with before she left. And anyway, you said they were seeing a counsellor; sounds like they were trying to work things out.'

'Mum just wanted to protect us. Like Millie said, the papers love a banking scandal. This was about the only place no one could get to us.'

'Mmm,' said Campbell.

'*What?*'

'Well, I just . . .' He drummed on his knees, like he was playing the bongos. 'Maybe you should talk to your sister.'

'You think I haven't tried?'

'Maybe you should try harder. If she's changed as much as you say she has, there's got to be a reason for it.'

Of course there had. I just wasn't sure I wanted to hear about it. 'OK. Next time I —'

'Come on,' said Campbell, jumping to his feet and offering me a hand up. 'I really think you should do this.'

'You mean *now*?'

'Wouldn't it be better to get it over with?'

'What about our date?'

He still had hold of my hand. I so didn't want him to let go.

'There'll be plenty more dates, Jess. At least, I hope so. Look, I don't want to come over all Dawdler on you, but we've got all the time in the world to get to know each other. Come on, I'll walk you back if you like.'

'No,' I said, reluctantly reclaiming my hand. 'Look, I will talk to her, but I need more time to think. Why don't you go and say goodnight to Winston? I'll stay here for a bit.'

Campbell shrugged. 'OK, if that's what you really want. I'll say . . . goodnight, then.'

The next bit should have been so easy, but we were both too chicken to step into the few centimetres of No Man's Land that separated us.

'We should do this again sometime,' I said.

'I'd like that,' said Campbell.

'And thanks for the flowers, they're . . .' I'd clutched them so tightly they were drooping inconsolably. ' . . . lovely.'

Campbell backed slowly into the shadows. 'Good luck with your sister, Jess. I really hope you get some answers.'

If I paced the cliffs any longer, my feet would carve out a permanent memorial.

Campbell was right; I should go talk to my sister.

Of *course* it was strange. I'd known that all along. Why would Mum just take off like that? OK, so she and Dad were going through a bad patch. That didn't mean we had to drive off in the middle of the night and abandon him.

But my talent for self-delusion was almost heroic. I'd accepted their lame explanations because I was too scared to think of the alternatives.

What were they hiding? More to the point, did I really want to know? Every time Millie hinted at something, I always backed off.

Dad once told me I should never be afraid of the truth. That was easy for him to say. Right at that moment it was the last thing I wanted to do.

But I couldn't stay on the clifftop forever. Even the wind was telling me to woman up and stop making feeble excuses. If Millie really knew something, it was time to find out.

Her
Fearful Symmetry

It must have been past midnight when I climbed through the entrance hatch, hoping in my palpitating heart that both of them were asleep. The connecting tube to Mum's room was pitch-black, but the flickering light at the end of the other tunnel meant only one thing. I muttered my expletive of choice and crawled towards it.

The 'vision' slowly materialised as my eyes grew accustomed to the light. She was sitting on the bed, a Mona Lisa smile hovering about her lips. At first, it felt kind of positive that she'd dumped her black sweatshirt on the floor. She wore that thing everywhere, even in bed. The pale blue T-shirt that once bore the slogan *Girls just want to have fun* was a massive improvement.

And then I saw what she was doing.

But Millie didn't see me; she was far too busy concentrating on her work, the knife poised in her tight white fist. It certainly answered one question anyway. I knew now what she'd been carving.

Herself.

My sister's once perfect arms were an abstract masterpiece of angry red lines.

But you know what was really scary? Even in her darkest hour, she hadn't forsaken the Golden One's passion for symmetry. Both arms matched perfectly.

The
Bad Thing

'What are you *doing*?'

She didn't even bother to come up with an implausible explanation. 'What does it look like?'

I grabbed hold of the chest of drawers and tried not to black out. 'But *why*?'

'Because it makes me feel better,' said Millie.

The nausea died when the anger took over. 'What, are you stupid or something? How can . . . hurting yourself make you feel better?'

'It's what I do when it all gets too much.'

'I know what self-harming is Amelia. Done the role-play, got the T-shirt. I just can't believe you'd be so selfish.'

'Selfish?' she whispered, gently weeping, like her freshly cut wounds. 'You don't know anything.'

Part of me wanted to comfort her, but the words spewed up from a reservoir of resentment deep inside. 'I know you've been a complete pain in the arse since we got here. Well, if you ask me, it's pathetic. The first bad thing that ever happened to the Golden One and you just can't hack it, can you? You think *you're* hard done by; what about the rest of us? Have you never stopped to think what all this is doing to Mum? And I can't even *begin* to imagine how Dad must feel.'

She rose slowly from the bed, looking me up and down like *I* was the lunatic, not her. 'Please don't make me do this, Jess.'

'Do what?'

She dropped the knife.

I dropped the flowers.

She opened her mouth. Not one sound emerged.

'Right, that's it. I'm telling Mum.'

'No, *don't*,' said Millie, swooping for her sweatshirt. 'She's got enough to worry about.'

'Oh come on, Mills,' I said, my anger swiftly dissolving into confusion. 'I can't just forget about it. What's Mum going to say when she finds out?'

She'd already shrouded the evidence in black cotton. 'She doesn't need to find out.'

'I don't know . . . I'm not sure, I mean . . .' The pod started spinning, like something out of an ancient sci-fi movie. 'If Dad was here, things would be different. He'd know exactly what to do.'

'You are joking, of course.'

'You've got stop this, Millie. It's been tough on all of us, but you can't keep blaming Dad.'

'Yes I can,' she said. 'You really don't know the first thing about him, do you?'

'I know he's not incompetent for a start. Brian said he was the best analyst he'd ever worked with. It's not Dad's fault if something went wrong with that Russian deal.'

Millie's laugh was a cross between the canned, American sit-com variety and an evil genius about to reveal her master plan. 'God, you're naive. Do you honestly think Mum would have dragged us off to the middle of nowhere if it was just about a couple of billion quid?'

'She wanted to protect us. That reporter was only the beginning. The media loves a banking scandal, you said so yourself.'

'Yes, but what do they love even more?' said Millie.

The pod stopped spinning. 'What are you . . . ?'

Actress tears, the size of pearls, were hurtling down her cheeks. 'They were all over his computer, Jess; thousands of . . . *vile* photographs. Kids, younger than you. He might be a great analyst, but he's a terrible human being.'

Maybe I'd heard wrong. Yeah, that's right, of course I had. 'Are you saying Dad's a . . . paedophile?'

'That's exactly what I'm saying. And he's not just been suspended, either; he's on bail until the trial. The sick bastard's only staying at Grandma's because he's not allowed anywhere near *us*.'

'I don't believe you.'

'Come on, Jess, don't be so dense. Why would I make it up?'

'Because you're a bloody liar,' I screamed, hurling myself at Millie and grabbing her arms where I knew it would hurt.

'Dad would never *ever* do a thing like that.'

She didn't even try to fight back, just whimpered like a coward and kept bleating 'Sorry'.

And I probably would have done some serious damage if Mum's sleep-starved voice hadn't trespassed into my nightmare. 'What on earth is going on in here? It's bad enough trying to sleep with that bunch of overgrown schoolboys outside.'

'You'd better ask *her*,' I said. 'I knew she had problems, but I didn't think she was a complete fantasist.'

Mum looked about a thousand years old. And it wasn't just for the lack of make-up. 'What are you talking about, Jess?'

'She's been telling disgusting lies about Dad.'

'She knows,' said Millie. '*I* told her. I'm sorry, Mum, I didn't mean to. It just came out.'

And suddenly Mum was crying too. She sleepwalked towards Millie, wrapping her arms around her in a soggy embrace. 'It's OK, it's OK. It's not your fault, love. I should never have asked you to keep quiet about it.'

I couldn't believe she wasn't angry. 'You mean it's actually true? Someone's been saying that Dad's a pervert?'

Mum nodded. 'I'm sorry, I should have told you.'

'Wait a minute,' I said, hoping against hope that I'd got it all wrong. 'Are you telling me you actually believe them?'

'I didn't want to,' said Mum, 'but the police practically dismantled the whole office when they came for his computer. And then they turned up at the house. They even took our wedding video.'

And now I was crying too. 'No, no, Dad's not like that, you know he isn't.'

The last thing I wanted was Mum's pity. 'It's not that simple, darling. Like Sue says, sometimes it's the people you least expect.'

'Yeah, well, she would say that, wouldn't she? The silly cow's had so many failed relationships it's no wonder she hates men.'

Millie was snivelling again. 'I'm so sorry, Jess. I really wanted to tell you.'

I'd had more than enough of their crocodile tears. 'You two are unbelievable.'

'Let's just sit down and talk about this,' said Mum. 'Come on, love, I —'

'Don't touch me. You make me sick, both of you. We were all he had. And you just left him to rot.'

'It's not like that,' said Millie. 'We only wanted to —'

'Sod off,' I said, unable to stomach another syllable of their sanctimonious whining. 'You know what your trouble is? You don't love him like I do.'

Mum's face was a watery mask of misery. 'Jess, please. Come back. You don't know . . .'

I shot down the tunnel, fumbled my way through the entry hatch and ran sobbing into the starry night.

Secrets
and Lies

Who knows where the next three days went? Sleepless and practically speechless, I wandered the island in a tear-filled trance.

Mum and Millie were forever trying to ambush me. I suppose I should have been grateful that they'd reverted to their old selves for a bit. Worrying about me seemed to have distracted them from their misery. Like slobbering journalists, they popped up everywhere, never fooling me for a minute with their two-faced smiles and pathetic invitations to talk. Like that was ever going to happen. What did they expect after filling my head with filthy lies?

Derek commented several times on my pale complexion and lack of 'oomph', but at least Campbell and the others didn't hassle me. They seemed content to let me dawdle behind them, and I was grateful they never once asked why I'd stopped coming to the Symposium or why I chose to spend my afternoons alone.

The truth is I felt sick. So sick that all I could keep down were a few sour apples from the orchard. My dad was the most honest man in the universe – and probably the kindest too. How could anyone think he was some kind of . . . ? I couldn't even say it.

But that wasn't the worst thing; the worst thing was the tiny voice in the back of my head that whispered *it might be true.*

There was no way of blotting it out completely, but it seemed to help if I stayed on the move. That's why I went walkabout, circling the island from noon till night in a desperate attempt to keep the voice silent. And sometimes on my travels I'd see Erika and the Junior Laggards, building sandcastles or flying paper kites. How I envied them their innocence. How I wished I could get mine back.

But if the days were long, the nights were longer. It was a blessing I could barely sleep, because in the rare moments when I just couldn't stop myself, the dreams that came were worse than any I'd ever known. Most of them started with that photograph, the self-portrait I'd sent to Dan Lulham. Except in my dreams, it wasn't the whole of St Thomas's Community College that was perving over it – it was my dad.

By the third night, I couldn't stand it any longer. Waking suddenly in a reservoir of my own sweat, I realised that the time had come. I *had* to talk to someone. But not just anybody; there was one person in the world who fitted the bill.

And I had a pretty good idea where to find him.

Winston grunted appreciatively, pressing his little pink face with the cute eye-markings against the wooden bars while Campbell scratched his back. It was the first time I ever felt jealous of a pig.

'Hi, Cam.'

I'd promised myself I wasn't going to cry for the next fifty years, but the look of concern on Campbell's face was enough to set me off again.

'Jess, I was so worried about you. Are you OK?'

'Couldn't sleep,' I sniffed.

'Neither could this poor guy. And I'm not surprised with all that noise.'

The men's voices were getting closer. Somewhere on the edge of the new forest, Earl was barking out orders. 'How dare you disobey me? You will do as I say!'

'Mind you, poor Winston wouldn't sleep a wink if he knew what my dad wanted to do to him.'

All *I* wanted was to throw myself into Campbell's arms. 'Look, I'm sorry I've been so . . . It's just that . . . well, I've had a lot on my mind.'

He seemed to read my mind perfectly. 'You talked to your sister, didn't you?'

'Yes.'

'And what did she say?'

'She said that . . . She said that . . .'

He took my hand, stroking it softly, like he was trying to

revive a sleeping princess. 'Want to talk about it?'

'I think so.'

The men were gathering outside the Symposium, their glowing torches filling the air with the scent of bonfire night.

'What are they *doing?*' said Campbell. 'They're supposed to be practising their survival skills.'

An argument was in progress. One voice cut above all the rest. 'Call yourselves men?' bellowed Earl. 'You don't know the meaning of the word. Looks like I'll have to show you myself.'

There was a murmur of protest before a solitary flame started crossing the field towards us.

'We can't talk here,' said Campbell. 'Come on, Jess. I know where we'll be safe.'

A cloudy curtain had descended on the stars, leaving the blackhouse in darkness. We stood face to face, like a couple in an Australian soap reciting their wedding vows. Lucky for me that I couldn't look into Campbell's eyes; it was hard enough telling him, let alone having to deal with his sympathy.

'But you know the worst part, don't you, Cam? It's not when some stranger says your dad's a pervert; it's when the people who are supposed to love him start saying it too. I thought Mum was stronger than that. I mean, according to her, running away was our only option. Can you believe it?'

Campbell's breathing quickened a little. 'No, of course not, but —'

'But what?'

'Well, it would kind of explain what your sister was doing. And I can see why your mum might have brought you here. That . . . sort of thing does tend to make the headlines.'

'Yes, but it's all lies,' I said. 'Dad would *never* do something like that. How could they even think it?'

'Well . . .'

'Well *what*?'

Campbell's breathing quickened a touch more. 'Maybe you don't know him as well as you think.'

'Not *you* as well.'

'No, I don't mean . . . I'm just saying that —'

'Forget it; I should have known you wouldn't understand.'

'But I *do*,' said Campbell.

I stumbled past him, groping desperately for the door. 'Well, you obviously don't.'

'Jess, *wait*. I need to tell you something.'

The crack in his voice made me hesitate. 'What is it?'

It was like one of those phone conversations where the other person doesn't talk for a long time and you think the line's gone dead. There was only a metre or so between us, but he sounded more distant than the stars. 'I thought I knew *my* dad too. Before we came here, he made a solemn promise that he'd never go back to his old ways. I believed him too. And then I found out he'd been lying to me.'

'How come?'

'There's this cave in the cliffs,' said Campbell. 'Right above Death Rock.'

It sounded like the kind of story Harry M would invent for Derek. 'What's that got to do with your dad?'

'Someone told me he was hiding a smartphone up there.'

'I don't think so, Campbell. Earl's pretty good for his age, but he's hardly going to climb a bare rock face for the sake of a mobile phone.'

'There's a path that leads down to it from the clifftops. I didn't want to believe it, but one night I followed him. He was in there for over an hour.'

'How do you know he wasn't meditating? That's what gurus do, isn't it?'

'I know exactly what he was doing,' said Campbell bitterly. 'He was playing online poker again. All that crap about technology and he was the one who couldn't live without it.'

'Why would he keep it in a cave? Why couldn't he just hide it in his sock drawer?'

'Too risky,' said Campbell. 'How do you think that lot would feel if they found out his "gift for prophecy" came courtesy of the online weather forecast? And anyway, Kevin said it was the only place on the island you could get a decent signal.'

'What's Kevin got to do with it?'

Campbell's voice receded even further. 'He was the one who told me about it. He said he wouldn't let on about Dad's gambling if I didn't tell anyone about *him*.'

'Tell them what?'

'That he was using Dad's phone to play *WoW*. Kev missed the internet more than any of us. You should have seen how happy he was when he made contact with his guild.' I couldn't see Campbell's face, but I knew for a fact he was tearing up. 'I just wish I'd said something. If I'd told one of the Dawdlers, Kevin would still be alive today.'

'I thought it was an accident.'

'It was,' said Campbell, 'but it didn't happen the way everyone thought. Kev must have heard Dad coming and panicked. He couldn't go back up the path, so he tried to go down instead. Well, *you've* seen how high it is. Poor Kev, he must have been . . .'

'Cam, *please* . . . Please don't cry. I know this is —'

'Dad even lied about that,' said Campbell. 'He told everyone Kev was recreating that ridiculous Crofter ritual.'

It was the most pitiful sound I'd ever heard; like the soundtrack to my nightmares – unworldly and not quite human. But whatever was making it, the heartbreaking squeal of terror that rose up from the valley seemed to sum up the situation perfectly.

'Oh my God,' I said. 'What was that?'

He didn't answer my question, but his voice was shrouded in pain. 'You see what I'm saying, Jess? Just because you love someone, doesn't mean they'll never let you down. Sometimes it's better to face up to —'

It was the only way to stop him.

Campbell didn't seem to object. I might have grabbed him first, but he was pretty quick to grab me back, whispering my name as we came together in the blackness.

And soon we were really kissing; angry, passionate kisses with perhaps a dash of desperation. It didn't stop me thinking how rubbish my life was, but for five minutes at least it deadened the pain.

1984

Mum and Millie were lying in wait when I got back. Cosied up on the beanbags, it reminded me of the old days and their irritating fondness for girlie chats.

'Jess, hang on a minute,' said Mum. 'I know you're upset, but this can't go on forever. I need to talk to you.'

'What is there to talk about?' I said, half hoping she could persuade me to stay.

Mum's voice sounded bleaker than ever. 'If we're going to get through this, we have to stick together as a family.'

'Well, it's a pity you didn't think of that when you abandoned Dad.'

'Jess, wait . . . That didn't come out right, you need to . . .'
I knew exactly what I needed. It popped into my head as I

scrambled through the connecting tube towards the bedroom. My *Where's Wally?* sports bag was in the bottom of the wardrobe. I wrestled open the dodgy zip and poured what was left of its contents onto my futon.

And there it was. Hard to believe that the heart-shaped plastic frame had seemed so awesome on my ninth birthday. That photo of Dad in the paddling pool always made me smile. He smiled back at me, little knowing that in the next few seconds Millie was going to creep up behind him with a bucket of cold water. Already I felt calmer. Dad was brilliant at that. He was good at saying the right thing, but unlike Mum, he was even better at knowing when to keep quiet.

'I miss him too, you know.' Millie was standing over me, looking down at Dad with her sad brown eyes.

'Does he look like a pervert?' I snapped. 'Well, does he?'

She sat beside me so that our shoulders were touching. I didn't pull away. 'I'd give anything for it not to be true, Jess. You know that, don't you?'

'You should have told me, Millie. You should have told me what they were saying about him.'

'Of course I should. Keeping it from you was the hardest thing I've ever done. I think that's why I wanted to, you know . . . hurt myself.

'You've got to promise me you'll never do something like that again.'

Millie nodded. Her tears were slowly licking away at my anger. 'Please don't hate me, Jess. I just didn't want you to get hurt.'

'I know,' I said. 'And I could never hate you, Mills. But I still don't believe any of that stuff about Dad.'

'No one's asking you to,' said Millie. 'I wish I could be so certain.'

Dad beamed at both of us as we hugged and whispered private apologies that I'd prefer to stay that way.

'What's this?' said Millie, sorting absently through the stuff I'd tipped onto the futon and picking out the plastic alien I thought I'd lost in Year Five. 'Didn't you used to collect them?'

'Horrible, isn't it?'

'These cartoons are pretty good though,' said Millie. 'Isn't that the really boring guy who came round for dinner once?'

'Brian Simkins,' I said. 'Hey look, he even gave me a card with his e-mail address.'

'Aren't you the lucky one?' said Millie, smiling at the picture of the world's dullest man riding the photocopier. 'Did *you* do these?'

'No, it was an IT guy from Dad's bank. I found them in his wastepaper basket when I was on work experience.'

'And what does this writing mean?'

'No idea.'

'No, wait,' said Millie. '*Todtnau* . . . I know that name. I'm *sure* I've heard it somewhere before.'

'It's no good asking me.'

'*Anyway*, what were you doing in the IT guy's wastepaper bin?'

'Long story.'

'Typical Jess,' she chuckled. 'I've missed you, you know.'

We weren't telepathic exactly, but I'm pretty sure we were thinking about the same person.

'And there's someone who's been missing you even more,'

said Millie. 'Why don't you go and talk to her?'

'I'm not sure if I'm ready,' I said, glancing down at Dad for guidance.

'She's hurting more than anyone,' said Millie. 'Go on, Jess. You know you want to.'

She was right there. And I knew exactly what Dad would say. 'OK . . . Fine.'

'I'll wait here for a bit,' said Millie. 'Give you two some time on your own.'

Mum jumped up the moment she saw me. 'Oh my, darling, are you OK? I was so, so worried about you.' Even without the comforting aroma of fresh towels and mango and papaya body butter, it felt good to be back in her arms again.

'I'm fine Mum . . . Honest.'

We sank into the purple beanbags like depressed synchronised swimmers.

'What have you been doing for the last three days? I know you haven't been eating, Jess. Maybe I could get you some bread or something?'

'I'm OK, Mum.'

'God, I've made a mess of this,' she said, running her fingers through her chronically tangled hair. 'You and your father, you were always so close. That's why I didn't want to tell you, Jess. I didn't think you could handle it. Stupid thing is, practically the first thing I did was to call Millie.'

'You know what she's been doing, don't you?'

Mum nodded. 'I only found out when you did. That was my fault too. I should never have asked her to keep a secret like that.'

'Will she be all right?'

'Yes . . . *Yes*. I'm sure she will,' said Mum. 'She's looking brighter already.'

I didn't want to ruin our reconciliation, but I needed to ask. 'So you really think Dad downloaded those photos?'

Mum pressed her teeth into her bottom lip. 'It doesn't look good, Jess. He was the only person who used that computer. And you know yourself he had his own office.'

'There *has* to be some other explanation, Mum. I'm certain of it.'

'Like what for instance?'

'I'm not sure yet,' I said, ashamed that a small note of doubt had crept into my voice. 'I just don't believe it, that's all.'

'Well, nothing's certain,' said Mum, who didn't seem to have so much as a semi-quaver in hers. 'We won't know for sure until after the trial.'

'And then can we go home.'

She stared at the space where the telly should have been. 'You know we'd been having marriage counselling, don't you? He was so wrapped up in his work. Perhaps I should have been more supportive.'

It was the million dollar question. 'Do you still love him, Mum?'

She had to think far too long. 'I'm not sure that he still loves me.'

'Of course he does. I know he does.'

'Well, sometimes it doesn't seem that way.'

This must be what it felt like, I thought, to have a mother who was more friend than probation officer. It had a lot going for it, but I saw now how the responsibility could do your head in.

'Anyway,' she said, her face slowly illuminating like an

energy-saving bulb. 'I hear you've got a new boyfriend. I hope he's an improvement on that Lulham boy.'

I always made it a strict policy never to discuss my private life with either parent. 'How do you know about Dan?'

'Millie told me. She said you were way too good for him.'

'Campbell's much better,' I said, suddenly aware of a warm glow on my sore red lips. 'You'd like him, I know you would.'

'As long as he hasn't got any tattoos,' said Mum.

It had been a long time since we'd laughed together. Millie obviously took it as her cue, emerging from the connecting tube with the IT guy's cartoons in her hand and a huge smile on her face. 'Mind if I join you?' she said, squeezing between Mum and me and draping her arms around us. 'Hey, Jess, that word, *todtnau*, I remember where I heard it now. It's a place in Germany, isn't it, Mum? Didn't you go there once with Dad?'

'Do you mind if we talk about something else?'

'Go on, Mum,' I said, 'I want to hear about you and Dad.'

Mum took a deep breath. If this was her chat show story, she wasn't exactly selling it. 'I think it was the summer of eighty-four. We were still students. David and I hitched down to Germany. You're right, Millie. Todtnau's a small village in the Black Forest.'

A *walking* holiday? That didn't sound like her at all. As for hitch-hiking, it was right up there with binge drinking and advertising your party on Facebook.

'It was the first time he said . . .' It was like someone had pushed her pause button.

'Come on, Mum. What did he say?'

'We were standing at the bottom of this amazing waterfall. He'd bought this bottle of plum schnapps, probably for Dutch

192

courage knowing your father. It was the first time he said . . .' Mum's eyes were clouding over.

Even Millie was getting impatient. 'Said what?'

'It was the first time he said that he loved me.'

It looked like Mum was about to sob her heart out; so how come she was laughing like a drain?

'What's so funny?' I said.

'It was your dad. You know what he's like. Just because he'd got German O-level he had to ruin the moment by giving me a lecture on pronunciation. "By the way, Maggie, it's pronounced Todtnau as in Tottenham Hotspur. The d is silent."'

Her Dad impersonation was spot on. I thought it was hilarious, but I couldn't help noticing that my sister looked kind of weirded out.

'What's the matter, Mills?'

'I don't get it,' she said. 'I mean, what was the name of a place that Mum and Dad visited nearly thirty years ago doing in the IT guy's wastepaper bin?'

Nature Dawdle
(part Two)

The next morning I discovered the architect of the heartbreaking scream that Cam and I had heard in the blackhouse. Winston was hanging by his trotters from a wooden scaffold outside the Symposium. I gazed at the pond of steaming crimson beneath his snout, fighting back the nausea and wishing I'd stayed in bed like Mum suggested.

'Don't look at that,' called Derek, struggling manfully to disguise his disgust. 'We're over here, Jessica. Come and join us.'

The Firewallers huddled gloomily in the morning mist, Naseeb and Molly deep in conversation whilst, hands in pockets, the boys prodded the ground with their non-descript trainers. Only Campbell stood alone, head bowed, his face buried in his hands.

Derek's voice sounded miles away. 'I said we're over here. Look, are you sure you're all right, Jessica? I meant what I said yesterday. If you're feeling peaky, maybe you should sit this session out.'

'I'm all right, thanks, Derek.' It was half true. At least I'd managed to keep breakfast down, and although I hadn't completely forgiven them, it felt good to be talking to Mum and Millie again.

But Winston's bloody carcass held me transfixed. Just a few hours ago he'd been snuffling around the sty without a care in the world. Life was like that – as I knew only too well.

'Come on,' said Lucy, taking my hand and leading me across to the others. 'Let's get you away from that thing.'

'How are you doing, Jess?' whispered Molly. 'You look more like yourself this morning.'

I was doing my best to stay positive. 'Yeah, I'm better thanks. Sorry if I've been a bit . . .'

'Forget it,' said one of the Harrys. 'Don't worry, we've all been there.'

Somehow I rather doubted it.

'Good to have you back on board,' said Jack.

But I still couldn't take my eyes off Winston. I'd seen it loads of time on television, but it was my first 'live' encounter with death.

'Gross, isn't it?' said Molly.

'And quite probably illegal,' added Naseeb.

'Poor Cam,' I said, my heart going out to the forlorn figure in the shapeless jumper. 'He really loved that pig. Who did it anyway?'

'Who do you think?' said Lucy. 'Earl wanted to prove

something. I'm not sure what exactly.'

Ed aimed a kick at the side of the Symposium. 'Told you he was a bloody nutter, didn't I?'

'Shhh,' said Lucy. 'Campbell's upset enough as it is.'

'It's not my fault if his old man's round the twist.'

Derek coughed to get our attention. 'OK, everyone. I know we were planning to start work on the fencing project this morning, but there's been a change of plan. I want you all to know that I was against this from the start.' He gestured vaguely at Winston, unable to bring himself to look. 'Perhaps we *are* too sentimental about our food, but in my opinion, Earl went too far. That's why today I want us to take a leisurely stroll around this beautiful island so that we can remind ourselves why we came here in the first place.'

There were no vintage expressions of delight as Derek voiced the possibility of sighting a family of otters or a young fulmar making its maiden flight. We trooped silently up the side of the hill towards the stone circle, the mood so subdued there wasn't even the hint of a smartarsed comment when I finally caught up with Campbell and slipped my hand into his.

'Are you all right, Cam?' It was the dumbest question since Aidan Corcoran's 'Why did Shakespeare turn the movie of *Romeo and Juliet* into a play?'.

His hand was cold and lifeless. 'I just don't get it. Why would he *do* something like that?'

'I don't know. It's —'

'Ed's right; he's off his bloody head. What am I going to do, Jess? I can't stay here.'

'Then you have to tell Earl that you want to leave.'

'I already have,' said Campbell. 'He told me I had no

choice. And that I should man up and get on with it.'

'He can't keep you here against your will.'

'What are you going to do, call the cops?'

Campbell's question went unanswered, much like the question in my head that was slowly starting to sound more reasonable: *Did Dad actually do it*? I'd told Mum there must be another explanation, but I'd spent the last three days trying and I was still struggling to come up with one. So that's what I was doing as we snailed our way towards the stone circle; going back over every detail of my work experience, racking my brains for anything that might help.

Sue's memorial for Kevin was finally in place. It looked like a random collection of driftwood with a few lines of poetry etched into it, but we gathered in a respectful semi-circle while Derek tried to identify the quotes.

'What about you, Jess?' whispered Campbell. 'How are things with your family?'

'Not that great. I just found out that my sister's been . . . cutting herself.'

'Oh Jess; I'm so sorry.'

'She'll be all right, she *has* to be. And at least we're talking again.'

Campbell squeezed my hand a little harder. 'And have you had time to think about your dad? I mean, whether he —'

'That's *all* I've been thinking about. He didn't do it, Campbell. I know he didn't.'

'Yeah, course,' said Campbell, sounding about as convincing as the dentist who promised me the injection wouldn't hurt.

'Right, let's get going, shall we?' said Derek. 'There's plenty more to see.'

It was nothing like my first nature dawdle; everyone else looked as miserable as I did. No one batted an eyelid when Derek thought he'd spotted a white tailed eagle, and even Derek himself sounded like a jaded tour guide going through the motions.

My optimism was slowly seeping into the hillside. It got so bad, I actually started picturing what life might be like at St Thomas's for the 'paedo's daughter': the backstabbing in assembly, giggling gaggles of Year Sevens pointing you out like a tourist attraction, graffiti in the toilets – not to mention the cowardly chorus of trolls.

And I was just imagining my first prison visit when the germ of an idea popped into my head. It wasn't exactly what Mr Catchpole would call a 'lightbulb moment', more like the distant glint of broken glass at the bottom of a deep loch. But at least it was something.

'Campbell?' I said, trying (and failing) to sound laid-back. 'How easy is it to hack someone's password?'

'It's certainly do-able,' said Campbell. 'There are various types of keystroke loggers – acoustic, kernel-based, hypervisor-based. You'd have to know what you were doing.'

'So, *in theory* it wouldn't be that hard?'

'In theory, I suppose.'

The mist was clearing by the time we hit the top of the cliffs. There really was something very special about the light. Whatever it kissed, you almost felt like you were seeing it for the very first time. The sky was unimaginably blue and the sea below a glistening combination of greens, whites and purples. But what was the point of the world being beautiful if the people living in it were so hideous?

Derek climbed onto a boulder, his tragic comb-over blowing in the wind, and tried to rally his demoralised troops. 'Just look at that view. Stunning, isn't it?'

But I wasn't really listening. I was thinking about something Millie said. *What was the name of a place that Mum and Dad visited nearly thirty years ago doing in the IT guy's wastepaper bin?* The glint at the bottom of the lake was definitely getting brighter.

'Now I know some of you may be a little bit . . . down in the dumps,' said Derek, 'but I always remember what my dear old English master, E B Smithies, said to us on the day he retired. He said that in spite of the challenges facing mankind at the end on the twentieth century, he was quite sure that things were getting better. And that whatever happened to us after we left school, it was always important not to lose sight of the big picture . . . Yes, Jessica?'

'Sorry, Derek. I am feeling a bit funny; terrible stomach cramps. Maybe I *had* better go and lie down.'

'I'll go with her,' said Campbell, 'just to make sure she gets back safely.'

'Yes, yes, of course,' said Derek. 'Perhaps you'd better pop into the surgery on the way.'

'Good idea,' I said, remembering what Miss Carver the drama teacher told us about people in real pain doing their best to conceal it, and going easy acting out the stomach cramps. 'I'm sure I'll feel better by tomorrow. See you then.'

Campbell propped me up as I speed-limped towards my first Oscar nomination.

'It's all right, Cam, you can stop now. They can't see us any more.'

'What's this all about?' he said.

'We need to talk to my sister.'

We found Millie outside the library, watching the Junior Laggards reading to each other from their new books. She looked so beautiful with the late summer sun in her hair.

'Aren't they the cutest?' she said. 'You used to be like that once, Jess.'

I was so out of breath I could hardly speak. 'We need to talk to you, Mills. It's really important.'

'Calm down,' she said, rubbing my back like she was trying to burp a baby. 'I'm Millie by the way. And you must be Campbell.'

Campbell blushed. Millie always had that effect on the opposite sex.

'So what's all this about, Jess?'

'It's about Dad,' I said.

Millie sighed. 'Are you quite sure you want to talk about this?'

'He didn't do it,' I said. 'I know he didn't.'

Campbell exchanged a dubious glance with my sister. 'I know that's what you want to believe,' he said. 'There just doesn't seem to be much evidence.'

'Well, how about this?' I said, pulling the crumpled paper from my back pocket and handing it to Campbell. 'I found it in the IT guy's wastepaper basket. You remember, Steve, the one I told you about?'

'Cartoons,' said Campbell. 'What that's got to do with anything?'

'Not the cartoons, the writing. *Todtnau*. It's a village in

Germany where Dad first told Mum he loved her. It's like you said, Millie. What was it doing in the IT guy's wastepaper bin? Well, I'll tell you what I reckon. I reckon it's Dad's password.'

'Then it's not a very good one,' said Campbell.

Millie clicked her fingers and pointed at me. 'That would make sense actually. Dad knows next to nothing about computers. It would be just like him to choose something like that.'

'You think so?' said Campbell.

'I *know* so,' I said. 'Steve the IT guy must have hacked Dad's password. How else could it have found its way into his wastepaper basket?'

Campbell looked distinctly underwhelmed. Thank God Millie sounded as thrilled as I was. 'I reckon you're right, Jess. And if the IT guy knew Dad's password, there was nothing to stop him logging on to his computer and downloading all that porn.'

'That's all very well,' said Campbell, 'but he'd still need time in your dad's office. You said there were thousands of images.'

By now I was on a roll. 'Friday lunchtimes, when Dad was at marriage counselling. He wanted to keep it a secret, but Steve must have known somehow. I even caught him messing about under Dad's desk. *That's* when he did it. All we have to do is check it out.'

Millie grabbed my arm just a bit too tightly. 'Listen, Jess; you mustn't tell Mum. Not until we know for certain.'

'I *am* certain,' I said. 'Dad's innocent. And this piece of paper proves it.'

Millie was suddenly looking very pleased with herself. 'It proves something else too. If Dad's password is the name of a place he and Mum visited nearly thirty years ago, it proves he still loves her.'

'Look, I don't want to be negative or anything,' said Campbell, 'but there's not a lot you can do about it, is there? It sounds like they've made their minds up. Even if we weren't stranded on this God forsaken island, I doubt there's anyone out there who'd believe you.'

I'd already thought of that. 'You'd think so, wouldn't you? But that's where you're wrong. OK, Campbell, here's what we're going to do.'

3G
Or Not 3G

Earl's cave reeked of a thousand years of bird poo. It wasn't the sort of place you found buried treasure in, but it didn't take long to locate the smartest smartphone I'd ever seen. It was lying at the bottom of a Hugo Boss messenger bag, with half a bottle of scruffing lotion, a solar charger and a battered copy of *Catcher in the Rye*.

Even by torchlight I could sense Campbell's disgust. 'I knew what he was like,' he said. 'Why did I ever think he could change?'

'He's your dad, Campbell. What else could you do?'

'I guess.'

It felt good to have a phone in my hand again. There was something so reassuring about the start-up tone, the way it gleamed fluorescently into life. Back home, we sometimes had to trek down to the bottom of the garden to get a decent signal. In a tiny cave, halfway up a cliff, on a remote Scottish island, it wasn't a problem. Thirty seconds later, I'd signed straight into my Hotmail account.

'And you're really sure you can trust this guy?' said Campbell.

I had to smile. It was the one thing I was completely certain of. 'Yeah, course.'

'You only get one shot at this, Jess. We can't risk coming back. God knows what my dad would do if he found out.'

'One shot is all I need.'

'Then you'd better go for it,' said Campbell.

There was assorted junk mail from my favourite cosmetics firms, seven Amazon recommendations, and even a couple of messages from Ella, who must have been wondering why I wasn't on Facebook. But all that would have to wait.

When Brian Simkins handed it to me, it was a miracle I didn't laugh in his face. But now, as I reached into my pocket and pulled out the index card bearing his disgustingly well-formed handwriting, it seemed like the most precious thing in the world. Selecting *New*, I tapped in Brian's e-mail address and started writing.

Once he knew about Dad's password and the dodgy IT guy, surely it was only a matter of time. As Dad said himself, *Brian is a man you can rely on, he may not be the most imaginative person in the universe, but there's no one better in a crisis.*

Clicking on *Send* was probably the happiest moment of my life. Not 'I just won Power Ballads Week on a TV talent show' happy, but truly, madly, deliriously joyful. 'OK, Cam,' I said. 'Mission accomplished.'

'Good,' said Campbell. 'Now all you have to do is *Delete history*, and then we can go.'

He looked much happier when we arrived back at the top of the cliffs. I took his arm and planted a sloppy wet kiss on his cheek. 'Thanks, Cam. That was brilliant.'

'No problem,' he said, poking his index finger through a hole in his jumper. 'The question is: what do we do now?'

'We wait, of course,' I said, surfing giddily on a tidal wave of excitement. 'It may not be tomorrow, or even the day after that, but trust me Campbell, we are getting out of here.'

On the Beach

Summer became autumn. And still nothing happened. I don't know what I expected exactly (a police helicopter, perhaps), but as the weeks dragged by, my impatience evolved into full-blown desperation.

It was the same with Millie. She'd improved so rapidly that, for a while, it was almost like having my sister back. We started taking long walks together. She showed me her favourite places on the island, and listened patiently while I yattered on about Campbell and the others. We'd even planned a menu for our first night back home. Just lately, though, her winning smile was frequently lost in thought. She hadn't been self-harming again or anything, and we still talked about Dad from time to time, but I was pretty sure she wasn't just worried about missing college, and I had this terrifying feeling I was in danger of losing her again.

The Firewallers were suffering too. We hardly ever played the game any more. Imaginary catalogue shopping was no substitute for the real thing, and talking about the old days seemed to make us feel worse. Harry M was developing an unhealthy obsession about having missed the summer blockbuster, Naseeb would have traded whole cities of souls for ten minutes on Facebook and Jack had this delusional fantasy about inventing a new app that would revolutionise the fast food industry.

But most of all, we missed our old friends. Perhaps it was a form of self-preservation, because we'd all tried not to think about them. Once we started, it was difficult to talk about anything else. Lucy had known Corrine since primary school. They'd even invented a secret language and a special punctuation mark for sarcasm (⊗). Ed got all nostalgic about a mate called Emmet who could fart 'God Save the Queen', and I couldn't help wondering what Ella was doing with her hair these days and who the hell she was hanging out with.

And it wasn't just the Firewallers. A delegation of senior Dawdlers had failed to persuade Earl that his 'back to nature initiative' was a step too far. He'd cancelled the two weekly delivery of extra supplies from the mainland and strict rationing was now in place. Even Sue admitted her beloved leader was 'not quite himself these days'. His late night saxophone playing (mainly Madness according to Mum, but I think she was talking about the band, not his mental state) meant we were sleep starved as well as hungry, and his shaggy beard gave him the appearance of an exiled dictator who'd been holed up in a cave for six months. Worse still, he was behaving like one. When

Harry M's family said they were thinking about leaving, he bawled them out in front of the whole community and refused to refund their deposit unless they stayed until Christmas.

Poor Campbell; all he really wanted was to go home. We still wandered up to the cliffs, and even kissed occasionally. But it felt more like a long goodbye. I knew I had to do something; the question was what? When the idea came to me, it sounded so crazy, I spent at least three days in denial. Danger is so not my friend that I would have done almost anything to avoid it. But there was no other way, and as the hours ticked by, it started to seem inevitable.

The more time that passed, the more I knew exactly what I had to do. It was just a case of finding the courage to go through with it.

What finally decided me was Mum. A pale, dejected copy of the strong, funny and oh so infuriating woman I'd loved, cried and battled with for over fifteen years, she was sinking faster than the Titanic.

I couldn't tell her what I was doing, of course, but I needed someone to break the news when it was too late for her to stop me. And it wasn't easy. Putting it into words would make it real. That's why I waited until the night before to share my secret with the two people I knew I could trust.

Millie said I was a 'total idiot', but at least she seemed to understand. Telling Campbell was the hardest thing I've ever done.

'It's been weeks now, Cam. Brian obviously didn't get the message. Or else they don't believe him. That's why I have to go myself. If I explain it all carefully, I know I can change their minds.'

'You've waited this long, Jess. Why not wait a little longer?'

'You heard what your dad said in the Symposium. Tomorrow's going to be the first calm day for weeks. If I don't go now, it could be too late.'

'It's still dangerous. That fishing boat is far too small. And what about the fog?'

'I've made my mind up, Cam. It's the only way.'

'What are you, mad or something?' said Campbell, wiping his eyes on the sleeve of his manky jumper. 'Please, Jess. I just don't want you to . . .' He grabbed hold of me, pressing his nose into the side of my neck and whispering, *'I love you so much.'*

And you know what? That was almost as scary as all the other stuff. It's not like no one had ever said it to me before. It's just that this time I believed him. And suddenly I kind of got it – the whole love thing. You see, he actually wanted what was best for me, not what was best for him.

'I'm sorry, Cam; I can't put it off any longer.'

Early the next morning, I pulled on that horrendous anorak for what I hoped would be the last time. Millie was just stirring as I slipped my *Where's Wally?* sports bag over my shoulder and climbed through the entry hatch.

Any worries I might have had about being spotted vanished in the mist. It was like a plague of white candyfloss that didn't even give you a sugar rush. I paid a final, nostalgia-free visit to the composting toilets and set off in what I hoped was the direction of the landing stage.

The distant sound of the Atlantic was fast becoming a

full-blooded roar, and the butterflies in my stomach a squawking flock of seagulls. Somewhere near the bottom of the snaky track leading to the beach, I got my first glimpse of the sea.

'Oh my God,' I whispered, suddenly realising that 'total idiot' didn't even come close.

Halfway down the beach, tethered to a post, was the little blue fishing boat I remembered from our arrival. I wasn't even sure I had the strength to launch it, let alone the know-how to get the outboard motor started.

But none of that mattered. Not for one minute had I lost faith in Dad – nanoseconds maybe, but certainly not minutes. Dad would *never* have given up on me and I wasn't about to let him down. Stumbling across the slippery pebbles through a wall of fog, rain and sea-spray, I managed to throw my sports bag into the back of the fishing boat and start untying her.

Next, the moment of truth. I ran round to the bow, grabbed hold of the towing rope and tried dragging the boat towards the sea.

She didn't move.

'Come on. Come on. Move, you stupid . . .'

You know that thing about parents being able to lift heavy objects off their children? Well, maybe children could summon up the extra strength to rescue their parents, because after a minute or so of fruitless heaving the reluctant vessel began inching forward.

'Yes, *yes*. Come on.'

The waves were rushing up the shore to meet me. Another ten metres or so and we'd be in business. But my heart sank when an angry voice rose above the racket of the elements.

'HOLD IT RIGHT THERE!'

I knew exactly who it belonged to. A moment later, a straggly beard emerged from the mist, attached to a man in a black leather raincoat who was striding across the beach towards me. But it wasn't the sight of Earl that stopped me dead in my tracks; it was the lonely figure limping along behind him.

'I'm so sorry, Jess,' said Campbell. 'I had to tell him. I couldn't let you do it. It's too dangerous.'

Earl had positioned himself at the stern. 'I always thought you'd be trouble.'

'Yeah, and I always thought you were a big fat fake.'

Earl reached instinctively for his love handles. 'You heard me. I forbid you to move.'

'You can't stop me,' I said. 'It's up to me if I want to go.'

'This island is mine,' roared Earl. 'I can do what I like.'

'Oh you think so, do you?'

Perhaps really loathing someone can make you stronger too. One massive tug and the boat started moving again.

Earl pulled in the opposite direction. 'Look, I'm warning you, young lady. There's only one way this is going to end.'

'We'll see about that.'

And I was actually winning until another voice pierced the mist with a desperate cry.

'JESS, NO!'

Mum was flailing down the beach, like a middle-aged fun runner who hadn't bothered to train for the marathon. Millie was miles ahead, gliding effortlessly, like a true thoroughbred. Even so, I could sense her relief as she grabbed my arm and pulled me towards her. 'Well, you didn't think I'd let you go through with an idiotic plan like that, did you?'

It was some time before Mum found the breath to speak. 'What in God's name do you think you're playing at, Jess?'

'Lucky for you I got here in time,' said Earl with a glutinous smile. 'She was planning to leave us. Of course I've explained that it's quite out of the question.'

But I wasn't done yet. 'Well, that's a pity, because if you don't let me go, I'll have to tell your Dawdler chums that you're not quite the man they think you are.'

Earl's smile slipped swiftly off the side of his face. 'What are you talking about?'

'I'm talking about that mobile phone you've got hidden away. How do you think they'd feel about their beloved leader if they knew all about his online gambling?'

'Well, you could do that,' said Earl, his slippery smile slithering back into place, 'but then I'd probably have to tell them about your poor father's little weakness.'

'You what?' said Millie.

'Yes, that's right,' said Earl. 'Sue told me all about him. You see, I know exactly why you came here. And I suppose it would be in the public interest for me to share it with everyone.'

'Dad, don't,' said Campbell. 'Jess's dad is innocent, anyway.'

'Yes, well, they all say that, don't they, son?' Earl rounded on me, flashing his smile like a movie villain's laser device. 'And the thing is, if you were to tell people about my "emergency telephone", there'd be nothing to stop me calling a couple of my old journo chums. I'm sure they'd love to know where you are.'

'You really are a piece of work, aren't you?' said Mum. 'How do you sleep at night? Oh that's right, *you don't*. You're always strangling that bloody saxophone.'

'It's your call, Jessica,' said Earl, his lips curling upwards into a self-satisfied smirk. 'Or rather *mine*, if you don't stop all this silliness about mobile telephones and come back to the pods.'

'Dad's innocent,' I said. 'I know he is.'

'Well, it's a pity no one else seems to think so,' said Earl. 'Now, can we get moving, please? Some of us have got communities to run.'

That was just about the lowest I ever came. Too low even to cry; I stopped fighting, and let the waves of disappointment flood over me. Funny how one of Mr Catchpole's favourite sayings should pop into my head at a time like that: *You've let the school down, you've let your parents down, but most of all, you've let yourself down.*

And I was about to begin the long trek back to the pods when Millie tugged at my arm and whispered, 'Jess, look!'

My sister's eyesight had always been better than mine. But what was she pointing at? And why was she crying and laughing at the same time?

We both laughed about it afterwards. If I'd have read it in one of the 'timeless classics' in the Dawdler library, I would probably have called it the 'father of all coincidences'. But none of that mattered when the ferry burst from the whiteness, like something out of a 3D movie and headed straight for the shore. At the helm was a bald man in a yellow cagoule. It was such a relief to see him that I almost forgave his crimes against literature and the four-legged detective who sometimes guest-starred in my dreams.

But the most glorious part of all was when the pale,

noticeably thinner figure seated at the bow rose shakily to his feet and waved at us. And if I live to a thousand, I'll never forget the moment he caught my eye and mouthed the words 'Thank you', nor the look of pure joy on Millie's face as she raced down to the water's edge and shouted, 'DADDY!'

Brave
New World

What more can I tell you? Chelsey never got her dream wedding. Steve the IT guy, on the other hand, got three and a half years for perverting the course of justice. He never really explained why he did it, but there were plenty of people out there who'd have paid serious money to make sure the Russian deal went through quickly. With Dad not around to ask difficult questions, that's exactly what happened.

It had taken Brian weeks ('and about half a furlong of red-tape') to convince the police they'd got the wrong man. Like Dad said, he wasn't the fastest worker in the universe, but if you're ever in real trouble, it's the Brian Simkinses of this world that you want fighting your corner.

* * *

We left Sloth the next day. A week later, Campbell and his dad followed. Apparently Earl never quite forgave the community for 'banishing' him, although he later admitted that under the circumstances it was probably for the best. The Dawdlers quickly disbanded, but Derek, Sue and a few of the others stayed behind to set up an exclusive tourist resort. It actually looks pretty good.

Revel in the stunning scenery and extravagant range of wildlife on a guided nature dawdle, take climbing lessons with a fully-qualified instructor, learn to meditate in the alternative therapy suite, release your inner J K Rowling under the expert guidance of our new writer in residence, or simply enjoy a smorgasbord of organic delicacies in the Symposium restaurant.

It's all on their website if you feel like checking it out.

I don't miss the island – well, not much anyway. It was kind of nice being outside all day, and even if the Dawdlers were a bit on the extreme side, some of the stuff they said has started making sense. That's why I persuaded Dad to install solar panels and why me and a girl called Ariel are setting up a school recycling plant. But most of all, I miss the Firewallers. Luckily, Naseeb set up a Sloth Survivors Facebook group so we could all keep in touch. Ed posts links to his highest scores on *MW3*, Molly's always blogging about the latest celebrity meltdown, Harry W (or is it Harry M?) is dating a girl called Kathleen and Jack's still working on his fast food app – which I'm sure you'll be hearing about very soon ⊗.

Of course, there was someone I wanted to be more than Facebook friends with. I'm not denying that Camden Lock market is amazing, but it turns out we've got so much more in common than just shopping. We're always texting, and even though we've agreed to disagree about tea tree oil, Lucy is one of my favourite people. (The highlights really suit her, by the way.)

Things are different at home too. I can't remember the last time Mum barged into my bedroom for one of her 'little chats'. In fact, she even asked for my advice about her and Dad.

And Millie's still a brilliant sister; she's just not the Golden One any more. Mum keeps a close eye on her to make sure she's not doing anything silly. She wasn't self-harming for very long, but those scars will be with her for life. The weird thing is, Mills seems to think that 'having a little wobble' was probably the best thing that ever happened to her. Apparently it's not easy when you're expected to be perfect the whole time. I wouldn't know, of course. She never talks about the island. But sometimes there's this funny incense smell coming from her bedroom, and I know she's sitting cross-legged in front of a scented candle with a look of fierce concentration on her face. What I'm not quite sure about is whether she's trying to remember or forget.

Mum and Dad were so awkward around each other after we got back that they were more like strangers. Dad couldn't understand why she'd shown so little faith in him and Mum kept telling me how frustrating it was trying to second-guess a man who refused to talk about his emotions. But at least he's not working so hard, and they've started seeing that counsellor again. I wasn't optimistic to start with, but a few days ago I thought I detected a glimmer of hope. You see, when Dad told his talking greyhound joke, Mum laughed like she was hearing it for the very first time.

Hang on a minute, I really need to take this.

'Hi, Cam – where are you? OK, text me when to get to the station. Yeah, can't wait. Yeah . . . Yeah, me too.'

That's Campbell. He's on the train. We've been going out for six months now, which is, like, a world record for me. Winchester's only about an hour away so we see quite a lot of each other. He's living with his mum now, but it looks like his dad has pretty much recovered from his breakdown. Earl's obviously decided he's better suited to the cut-throat world of advertising than running an eco-community. Watch out for his new toothpaste advert – Cam says it's amazing.

And what about school? Well, school's school, isn't it? Dad's story was old news by the time I went back, but I still was kind of nervous about it. Ella didn't exactly help matters. The first thing she said when I walked into registration was, 'Don't worry, babes, we've all forgotten about that photo.' But I guess I'm more confident now, so I just laughed.

I try not to think too much about our time on Sloth, only sometimes I can't help it. Like the other day in PSHE. Mr Catchpole was hosting a quiz on the different types of skin cancer, so I slipped in my earbuds, closed my eyes and tuned out to my favourite track. And suddenly I was back in the Symposium, sitting cross-legged with a force nine gale up my bum.

Next thing I knew, old Catchpole was standing over me demanding my iPod. 'Thank you, Jessica. I'll have that if you don't mind. What ghastly aberration are you punishing your eardrums with anyway? Something intellectually stimulating, I'm sure.' ⊗

It's a pity I couldn't put it on YouTube for future generations of St Thomasites to wonder at, because you really should have seen the look on his face when he heard my reply.

'That's right, sir. It's Alfred Cortot's legendary 1929 recording of Chopin's waltz in C sharp minor.'

piccadillypress.co.uk/teen

Go online to discover:

☆ more books you'll love

☆ competitions

☆ sneak peeks inside books

☆ fun activities and downloads

☆ Find us on Facebook for exclusive
competitions, giveaways and more!
www.facebook.com/piccadillypressbooks

☆ Follow us on Twitter
www.twitter.com/PiccadillyPress